LOST SOULS

Pat & Christee,

Hope you enjoy it.

[signature]

Cover design by Bill Toth
Book design by Iris Bass
Author photograph by Paul Shambroom

LOST SOULS

ANTHONY SCHMITZ

AVAILABLE
PRESS

BALLANTINE BOOKS • NEW YORK

An Available Press Book

Copyright © 1988 by Anthony Schmitz

All rights reserved under International and Pan-American Copyright
Conventions. Published in the United States of America by Ballantine
Books, a division of Random House, Inc., New York, and simultaneously
in Canada by Random House of Canada Limited, Toronto.

Library of Congress Catalog Card Number: 88-91123

ISBN 0-345-35722-1

Manufactured in the United States of America

First Edition: October 1988

SUNDAY

DO YOU KNOW HOW I FEEL?

Put your car up on blocks and floor the accelerator and listen to the engine whine. I'm not going anywhere but my mind is always racing. Most times my forehead is hot to the touch. It's been that way ever since I broke my hip.

It was the spring before last, a night that set even blood as ancient as mine pounding. The apple trees in the orchard outside my window were in bloom, the pale pink flowers just visible in the dark. The breeze, so soft and warm, carried the sound of cows groaning in their sleep. In the cemetery the lilacs bloomed, their scent mixed with that of grass and the black dirt.

I had tossed for hours, which is nothing new. I get to thinking about who said what and what I said back and what I should have said and then before I know it I'm still staring at the ceiling and it's three o'clock. That night I turned from my back to my side to my stomach, over and over, a whirling dervish. I prayed. I stewed over old gossip. And then, weighing the odds of falling asleep against the probability of losing my mind, I pulled on my shoes and walked to the orchard, more awake than I had been all day.

The orchard is the quietest place in town, an admittedly fine distinction to make in a place the size of St. Jude. The low-hanging branches and thick leaves and the grass that

1

grows long around the tree trunks—they deaden everything except the wind. The leaves whispered.

In my orchard I know every clod of dirt, every bend of the branches. When a limb breaks I'm bereft. If a sapling survives I rejoice. In summer the red fruit shines darkly in the moonlight, in fall the last brown apples rot into the earth, in winter the trees are black sticks in the snow. I see the orchard in one season and I imagine it in all the others.

I walked among the smooth-skinned trees, through the pasture that ends against the cemetery's wrought iron fence. The graves stood in the black grass, huddled beneath a grove of evergreens.

Schmitt, Schmabel, Raun, Braun—one German name after another is carved in the stones. They settled in St. Jude because the landscape is Bavarian. The hills roll down into valleys where slow, muddy rivers flow, and the woods grow thick and dark, and the seasons change from the impossibly hot days of summer, when not even the flies can bear to move, to winter nights so cold that the snow screeches underfoot. These poor Germans moved across an ocean to end up in the same place! Now the names slowly erode from their tombstones, and even I have trouble remembering all the faces.

The streetlight died in the apple trees. The moon had not yet risen. I could barely see my feet, but what of it? I know every step by heart. In the night I could look toward the grocer Lieber's tombstone and see him again, his face scarlet as he unloaded a truck full of melons. When I passed the plot of Mrs. Moon, my old housekeeper, the smell of melting butter rose from the dirt. My memory filled the cemetery, bringing the dead back into the spring night where everything ached to grow. I felt even the worms burrowing under my feet, thousands of worms working through the soil, loosening it for the year's new growth. Everything felt alive, which was not quite the case.

Two days earlier Jack Thiesen got his arm yanked off while working on a hay baler. He bled to death alone in his barn. His son found him that night, sitting with the mangled limb in his lap and a stupefied look on his face. Jack was laid out at the funeral home, a healthy-looking corpse. I fell into his grave.

Most likely you've never fallen into a grave, so stop and consider what I'm saying. There's nothing halfway about it. The hole is cut straight down and the dirt is black, black, black, and the earth swallows you whole.

I clawed at the grass but that didn't slow me down. I fell and my hip shattered. The pain was a white light behind my eyeballs, searing. *I am the light*, that's what He says. You understand the direction my thoughts were headed. But then the light dimmed and the pain settled into a dull, secular throb. The Lord knows I screamed for help—I screamed until my throat was raw—but there wasn't a soul to hear. I squeezed the wet clay in my fists and cursed.

The stars swirled above me. A wisp of tree root worked its way into my ear. The moon cut through the narrow slit of sky in my view, and then the night turned black again.

It occurred to me that I was eye-to-eye, more or less, with Jack's dead wife, who was buried to my left, and Jack's dead infant, who lay another few feet to the right. I had forgotten just how much bad luck poor Jack had suffered, and I felt much better for remembering.

Years earlier Jack and I stood over the baby's cradle together, praying for just a thimble of the Lord's mercy after his infant caught God-knows-what and coughed and cried for days on end. His wife sang the same lullaby over and over, an eerie tune straight out of the Black Forest. She refused to pray, saying it was no use praying to a God who struck down babies. When the melody came back to me at the bottom of Jack's grave I hummed it, and my eyes filled with tears from the memory and the pain.

I heard Jack's baby crying. Not just remembered the sound but heard it. Then I heard that lullaby exactly as Jack's wife sang it, so clear and devilish that it could not have been memory alone. I closed my eyes and saw her again, dry-eyed, burning with love and despair and hatred. The first birds sang, too, and the music filled the night. And me, I lay like another clod of dirt at the bottom of the grave, the root in my ear hinting at the future.

The stars disappeared. The sky turned turquoise. Bright sunlight shone in a halo around a man's body. The voice I heard was rich and deep.

"What are you doing down there?"

I didn't see a shepherd's crook, and the hair seemed awfully short, but there is no telling about these things. I said a quick prayer, repenting for, well, don't get me started.

When my eyes focused I recognized the ignorant face that looked down at me. "Get me out of here, Tottenberg," I cried. The young undertaker shouted for help. I wet my pants and fell into a feverish sleep. That day my hip was fit with a new ball and socket.

The minute my Medicare ran out I was transferred to this home for aged, drunk, and crazy priests.

WHERE WAS I?

Sch . . . Schn . . . ? Schnee? Towering drifts of it and me, black-robed and frozen, at the bottom. Feel my fingers—they're already cold. Circulation, the doctor says.

Schnid?

No, no, no.

Schneider! That's it. Schneider.

Watch this.

"Schneider!"

Ha. Every time I yell he's jolted. His face registers surprise and dismay simultaneously; he looks like a man about to drop from a heart attack. Believe me, I know.

I've watched people die from anything you can imagine: women in childbirth, men fallen from steeples, farmers dragged by tractors, and kids pulled from deep water. I've knelt beside them all, muttered a few prayers, and felt their souls slip away. Go ahead and laugh, but I tell you it's true. Most people don't see enough of death to recognize its finer points. They're too busy digging for their handkerchiefs to feel the warm shudder of a soul set free.

Now watch Schneider fold his paper and straighten his collar. The boy is as constant as the stars. "Yes, Father," he says, looming over my wheelchair.

Why exactly did I call him?

I must have had a reason, but I cannot for the life of me recall what it was. The nurses here whisper, "Poor man, his mind is going." But that's not it at all. Why should I remember? One day is the same as the next. I sit and sit and then sit some more, staring at the same pack of doddering fools. The distant past is infinitely more interesting than the last five minutes.

Take a look around and you can see what I mean. Old Drake there, his mouth hanging limp, a thread of spittle dripping to his chest. McConnell, who squints through his thick brows and chants naa-aaa, naa-aaa, naa-aaa day and night. Schmidt, whining to anyone who will listen, "I'm for the wind. I'm ready to blow away. I'm for the wind." And thirty others, all arranged in the day room like potted plants, drooping and drooling and gagging ahead of the television set, all of us tied into our wheelchairs so we don't ooze onto the floor.

"Father?" Schneider says again. I have to tell him something.

"Drake," I say. "It's Father Drake. Close the man's mouth."

Drake. Better drool than the nonsense that used to escape from him every Sunday. Old Drake, who pleaded to preserve the Latin mass. Drake, who fought so that his parish could continue to have no idea what he said. I never planned to pity him, and yet I do. These days I don't look so good myself.

Honestly, I'm nearly as concerned about Schneider. Such a healthy, strong boy! Such a blank face! He's like a cow, happy to chew over his paper hour after hour. I hate to see him idle. He can move but he'd rather sit. I'm four times his age and there is more energy in my little finger. What I wouldn't give to have Schneider's legs! It must be saintly, don't you think, to force him to use those talents the Lord gave him.

Schneider studies me, studies Drake, then walks over to

the wheezing old priest. He places one finger on the tip of Drake's chin and pushes gently upward.

"*Domine patri*," Drake mumbles from his stupor, mistaking Schneider's smooth cheeks for something less earthly. Cherubim is more like it. Schneider's face glows with ignorance. Drake falls asleep again in an instant.

Schneider examines his finger. He wipes the old man's dribble against his trouser leg and goes back to his paper. And I sink deeper in my chair, waiting, waiting, waiting. Waiting for what? I search the room full of living dead, looking for another situation requiring Schneider's attention.

I'M NOT UTTERLY ABANDONED IN THIS PLACE. I HAVE A nephew in Wisconsin who visits once a month. He comes alone: I suspect his wife has decided I'm his problem, not hers. We talk about the weather, about his children. What about birth control? I ask, hoping he'll rise to the bait. What about married priests? He rubs his temples and tells me about a snowstorm in the Dakotas. He fears I'm looking for an argument. Of course I am.

He always brings a cake, the fruit of his wife's guilt. I can't complain; it beats the baby food we're served here. My nephew sets the cake on my lap, hands his camera to a nurse, and insists that she snap our picture. Next month he hangs the developed photo on my bulletin board. They're all the same. I look wide-eyed at the camera, frosting smeared across my lips. The gaudy cake I hold seems to mock me. My nephew, skin stretched tight with the extra thirty pounds he carries, stands behind my wheelchair grinning like a madman. I hate these pictures; they lay bare my absurd helplessness. But I don't dare take them down.

What if he takes offense? What if he never returns?

LOOK AT SCHNEIDER NOW. HIS HAND FLUTTERS AROUND HIS ear as he directs his little finger into its crevices. Schneider is assigned here as part of his seminary studies, for practical experience in comforting the afflicted. Comfort is not even half of what I need. For decades I was at the center of the universe. My parish was a small universe, granted, but it all revolved around me.

"Is there anything else you want to confess?" That was the only oil I needed to lubricate the great wheels of guilt. Sins of commission, sins of omission, sins of envy, pride, and lust. I heard them all. I blessed marriages, I baptized children, I buried the dead, and I turned wine into blood. And now I fill my day watching Schneider pick at his ear.

"Schneider!" I shriek.

He responds, therefore I am. Shock, then exasperation, then he hulks over to me once more.

"Schneider," I say, "let's take a Sunday drive."

He should have more backbone, but then if he did I couldn't shanghai him on his day off. "Where to, Father?" he says, looking like an overstuffed St. Francis.

"Let's take in a mass. Let's see what's happening in old St. Jude."

And he nods, his expression that of an about-to-be mar- tyred saint. What a lot of white bread the Lord calls to the cloth these days! I should be thankful. Weak link that he is, the boy is my only connection with the world outside.

Saturday night I cannot keep my eyes closed, let alone sleep. When Sunday morning arrives—Gloria!—I take up my vigil in a wheelchair at the nursing home door. Both hands gripping my cane, I scan the parking lot for young Schneider.

What if he forgets? What if he calls with some lamebrain excuse? I will burst my seams, I will simply explode. I shake until he turns the corner at exactly eight—praise Jesus!—and loads me into his battered Dodge.

We poke through the suburbs, their names like honey on my tongue. Eden Prairie, Golden Valley: that is exactly what they were when I first saw them. A prairie of corn hemmed in by oak and elm, a valley filled with wheat bent by every wind. I ignore the hamburger stands and car lots that stretch along the freeway now. I close my eyes and imagine what was.

With the first open pasture I am resurrected. The fields are still wet with last night's rain. The earth is black as my cassock. Corn and soybeans break through the dirt and the green rows stretch over the hills. A herd of holsteins lounges on a mound of grass. Oh, my heart is about to break.

Schneider, callow nitwit that he is, answers a question I don't recall having asked. "After I'm ordained, you know, I'm hoping for a small parish in a small town. I want to minister to, like, the total community."

God help the faithful. The boy's got a textbook for a brain. When a man's wife is dead and his child is sick and his crops have died in the field, what exactly will he do? Recite Augustine's theory of God's goodness?

"Have I ever told you about my first assignment, Schneider? Right out in St. Jude?" A dullness in his expression tells me that I have, but no matter. He needs all the help he can get.

Schneider's eyes are fixed on the road. I crane and twist in my seat. I want to see everything: the sagging barns, the oak ringed by sumac, the fishing boat that rots on a certain hill. In comparison, Schneider is blind.

I start my story. Which, if I do say so myself, is a fine story for a Sunday drive. It's a love story, at least up to the point where it gets tangled up in death and lies.

Schneider, impatient already, steps on the gas.

WAS IT FIFTY OR SIXTY YEARS AGO? NEVER MIND. I WAS AS young and sinewy as Schneider, right out of the seminary and ready to set the world straight. My assignment was St. Jude, a town I had never seen.

"A plum," the bishop's assistant explained. He was that type of cleric who is polished smooth, sexless. I didn't ask him why, if St. Jude was such a plum, I was being sent there. I didn't ask anything at all, except when I could start.

"Sunday, this Sunday," he said. "A wonderful lake. Surrounded by farms. People used to pay to go there. A tourist town." He blabbered merrily as he led me to the door, then clapped my back and sent me off, a blissful ignoramus. I returned to my dormitory room barely aware of how I got there.

The day before I set out a letter reached me from St. Jude. My room was already stripped. My bag waited, packed at the foot of the bed.

"My dear Father Hoven," the letter began.

Intoxicating greeting!

"Could you be so kind as to prepare a few words for the ten o'clock mass? The parish is of course eager to hear from you, just as I am eager to put its care in your hands." The signature, jittery and crabbed, seemed to read "John Hunger."

Could Father Hoven trouble himself to prepare a few words? Would the birds be so kind as to fly? I shut the door to my cell and worked through the night, covering the floor with blossoms of crumpled paper. Early the next morning I harvested three smudged sheets filled with tiny print.

I don't remember the exact words anymore, praise Jesus. Or—this is closer to the truth—I've made an effort to forget. In general I suggested that while there was much I must learn I was nobody's fool, that despite my age I was ready to take charge, that together we would walk the path of the Lord. Idiocy, in a word.

At dawn I folded the sermon and tucked it deep in my breast pocket. By then the paper was a close cousin to Moses's burning bush, warm to the touch. I picked up my suitcase and crept through the dormitory, my footsteps hollow in the bare halls. Down the stone stairs, through the dingy lounge, then out the door that slammed as finally as a sepulcher.

I stood on the seminary green. The first light filtered through the maples. A trolley waited on the street. Free at last, I told myself, though the opposite was closer to the truth. I hurried across the dew-stained grass.

The train station was cool, gloomy, immense. A breeze swept around the pillars carrying soot from the idling trains. Except for a ticketing agent the place was empty.

I fingered my ticket. I patted my coat pocket to check for my sermon. I strained to imagine my bleating flock.

A black-suited conductor shouted "Attention!" as though a crowd waited, not just me. He sang out a list of names—"Excelsior, Eden Prairie, Victoria"—each stop sounding happier than the one that preceded it. When he called "St. Jude" he bent the two syllables into a song.

"All aboard," he bellowed. I rushed toward the gate.

His greasy mustache pinched his nose as he laughed. "Ja, the new priest for St. Jude!" These words had a melody, too—the man was incapable of simply speaking. His teeth were crooked, and his smile was not entirely friendly. He pulled a gray handkerchief from his pocket and dabbed his eyes.

"Catholic?" I asked.

"Not exactly," he said. "But I tell you anyway, a priest has plenty to do in St. Jude." He leaned toward me, a conspirator. "Just last summer. That tornado. Lifts a cow up and throws it through the church window. Carries a nun up to heaven or who knows where. No body ever found. And it doesn't touch nothing else." He pushed his face close to mine and whispered, "I say it's a sign."

I fumbled for my ticket. Without giving it a glance he jammed the slip in his pocket, his eyebrows twitching.

Crazy, I thought. A sign. So which of the Wise Men is he?

"All aboard," he yelled again. I was the only passenger in a gloomy wooden car that stank of sweat and cigar smoke.

The train pulled away from the station, tracing the river. It passed under a half-dozen bridges, skirting black mountains of coal stored in the riverbanks. Then the track broke away from the river, past a brewery and on through a tangle of railroad housing. The train climbed out of the valley, onto higher ground where the sun seemed brighter.

I saw corn, acres and acres waving green in the wind. I was on my way to St. Jude. Lips moving silently, I preached my sermon to the herds of cows that stared dumbly at the train.

The tracks followed a stream that cut deeply into the hills. The trees closed in on us, a green canopy that blocked off the sun. I dozed restlessly, dreaming of myself thundering from a marble pulpit. As the train shrieked through a turn I woke.

To the right a lake shone silver and blue in the morning light. Two steeples and a water tower rose through the trees on the far bank. The train followed the water's edge, stopping beside a wooden depot badly in need of paint. A sign nailed to the clapboard read:

ST. JUDE
PARADISE OF THE MIDWEST

I had barely set foot on the platform when steam hissed from the train brakes. The wheels started to turn again.

The conductor's voice boomed over the growling engine. "Don't forget to pray for me," he shouted, flashing his yellow teeth and laughing. I stood alone on the platform as the train disappeared.

SHE REMINDED ME OF A WELL-FED CHICKEN. HER HAIR WAS white, except for a few strands of dull red. Her nose was hooked, her eyes pinpoints.

"Father Hoven!" she called, hurrying toward the platform. "We got to hurry! Church is in an hour!"

"I'm Father Hoven."

"Who else would you be?"

"I don't know."

"I suppose not." She eyed me suspiciously. "I'm Mrs. Moon," she said finally. "The housekeeper at the rectory. Breakfast is waiting."

She did not walk so much as waddle, but she waddled very quickly. We climbed a hill to the treeless main street, then turned left past a gas station, a plain clapboard hotel, a bakery, a hardware store, and a pharmacy. The buildings, one-story brick for the most part, seemed crushed to earth by the vast sky.

"What a lovely town," I said, my first lie in St. Jude. Main Street was sunstruck, desolate. The streets were too wide, the buildings too low. The place lacked shadow.

"Ach," Mrs. Moon replied, not bothering to turn around. "We should have eaten fifteen minutes ago."

I chased her around another corner and then stopped dead in my tracks. The church—my church!—stood at the end of the block. The golden brick soared toward heaven, the steeple top so high I craned my head to take it in. In the churchyard young apple trees swayed in the breeze, gangly as young girls.

Mrs. Moon glanced back and shook her head. She charged toward the rectory, unable to wait. I let myself in.

"Hello?" I called.

"It's him," I heard Mrs. Moon say.

"Father Hoven?" The voice was tired, undernourished. I heard slippers drag across the wood floor.

"Father Hunger?"

The priest who appeared seemed barely capable of making himself heard in the next room, let alone the next world. His cassock hung loose from his shoulders. His collar was too big and his head too large and his hair a wispy gray. "Unger," he said. "James *Unger*. You got my letter?"

Unger clutched the doorpost to steady himself. Mrs. Moon peered out from the kitchen. I realized, suddenly, *This is mine*. This house, the church, the souls beyond its walls. It's all mine. I stood there dumbly, unable to speak.

"I was afraid of that," Unger said.

"No," I said finally. "I have it. The sermon I mean. Right here."

I pulled the sheets from my pocket. He turned over the pages, squinting at the text. "I'm sure you'll find the parish more patient than I have," he said, distracted.

He led me to the dining room door, pointing me toward a seat. Mrs. Moon dashed back and forth, laden with serving bowls. A barbaric amount of food was spread across the table. I was awestruck. No priest I knew save Unger dared eat or drink past midnight on a day when he said mass.

"Are you eating or not?" Mrs. Moon said. I couldn't decide what answer she wanted.

"It's all right?" I asked Father Unger.

He picked at a bowl of stewed tomatoes. "You're going to make Mrs. Moon a very happy woman," he said, not quite answering my question. I sat and started to fill my plate. Mrs. Moon pushed through the swinging door from the kitchen with a coffeecake and applesauce and a picnic ham.

"Mrs. Moon believes the world's problems are due to bad eating habits," the priest said. "Which is likely as true as any other theory."

"Well . . ." He waited for me to finish. "You're leaving a beautiful place," I said.

"You think so?"

"The lake. The farms. The town."

"Well, I suppose it seems that way."

He stirred his coffee and sighed.

"You really should know. But then I shouldn't cloud your thinking. Of course you'd find out yourself eventually." He looked over my shoulder, out the window.

"Excuse me," I said.

"I've been here ten years. Long enough to draw some conclusions. Allow me one observation about this beautiful place.

"These people came from a forest and moved to another one and for all I know they worship trees. If they hear a dog bark in the night they're sure it's wolves. Once they've heard their wolf then they're sure it waits for them. And the wolf is not a wolf but evil itself. Nothing happens by accident or by the hand of God. They reach for their rosaries not from faith but from superstition. I appears to be Christianity but it isn't."

"I heard a story already," I said, eager to please. "About the tornado and the nun."

Father Unger crossed himself.

"Sister Agnes. Bless her. She went out to gather the wash before the rain. A funnel dropped from the sky. No one expected a tornado. She was swept away. The linens fell as she ascended. We found her habit in the lake. And the convent cow went right through the church's stained glass. The animal broke five pews and its own neck. A tremendous mess."

Mrs. Moon poured me coffee. "The devil's work," she hissed. Father Unger pretended not to hear.

"I'll tell you what the problem is," he said. "They expect the worst. They wallow in bad news. If one of their neighbors is stricken—cancer, fire, flood, whatever—they're momentarily content. 'Now he knows how the rest of us have it,' they say. For the longest time I could not begin to understand it."

"And now?" I said.

"I've been ill myself," he said, waving a hand over his thin frame.

"I don't see."

"I'm afraid you will," he said, pushing his chair away from the table. He pulled himself to his feet and shuffled out the door.

"Maybe now we have a priest who's religious," Mrs. Moon muttered. She scowled at the fork I held. "You're done with that," she said, pulling away my plate. "Go on now. You don't have all day." I surrendered the fork to her and hurried after Father Unger.

TWENTY MINUTES LATER, AFTER THE ALTAR BOYS STUMBLED through a pig latin version of the Confiteor and the choir wailed a Kyrie, I climbed the pulpit steps. My stomach gurgled, the worn boards creaked.

I stared out and the citizens of St. Jude stared back. What a strange lot they were! Farmers, their necks brown as coconuts and their skulls white as their Sunday shirts. Their wives, thick as oaks growing from the church floor. Dozens of jug-eared kids, all squirming, drooling, whimpering. Eight nuns, an army of the aged, and the light of the angels spread over it all, morning light filtered through a thousand panes of stained glass.

They had a look of groggy resignation, their eyes all gone dead. Later I found it liberating—if no one heard me it made no difference what I said. But that morning sweat flowed from my brow and eddied around my collar.

As a began a dozen dull eyes closed tight as Lazurus'. A farmer in the front row picked at a wart. His son explored his nose. A high school girl tugged at a hangnail. What a quantity of flesh was squeezed and scratched! Even the nuns seemed to go cross-eyed. Unger coughed, a gurgling wheeze. A farmer crushed a fly against a pillar with his missal.

"I'm like a seed planted in this soil," I said, finally. "Waiting to grow with the place even as I provide it spiritual nourishment." The congregation, slowly realizing I had finished, struggled to its feet again and yodeled a hymn.

Father Unger looked right through me as I stepped down, a vague smile on his gray face. "Bless you, son," he whispered.

He raced through the rest of the mass, the Latin an unintelligible mumble. He swiped at the air—a final blessing—and walked wearily toward the door. I stood my ground, waiting for the suffering in the choir to end.

Back in the sacristy Unger's vestment was draped across a chair. Mrs. Moon bustled in, picked up the robe and shook it.

"What happened to Father?" I asked her.

She shrugged. "I'm done worrying about him," she said.

I went outside to shake hands, standing in the shade of a giant elm near the side door. The girls blushed, the men pumped my hand and mumbled, the women glanced at me quickly and then huddled with their neighbors again. I returned to the rectory inspired by a cockeyed notion: I was ready to do God's work.

Father Unger packed his bags that afternoon and left on the four o'clock train. The parish of St. Jude was mine alone.

MONDAY

SCHNEIDER HASN'T SAID ANYTHING IN FIFTEEN MINUTES. His jaw hangs loose and his eyelids droop. Does he hear a word I say?

"Can't drive with your eyes closed."

I jab him. My fingers are twisted, gnarly, like the roots of an old tree. He jerks the car away from the ditch.

"Why did Father Augur leave?" he asks, yawning.

"Auger? Am I boring you, Schneider?"

"Huh?"

"Unger!"

"Oh, right."

"I know I'm right."

Schneider stares sullenly at the road.

If I could afford to be patient I'd ease up on the boy. He's like a dull-witted dog; well meaning, I suppose. But the blood I hear pounding in my ears, it's the same as a clock's ticking. I can't waste a second. Yet each day contains more hours than I know how to use. I'm bored and anxious all at once.

"Let me tell you this, Schneider. If Unger had stayed I wouldn't be here now. Think of it. My whole life, changed by someone else's decision."

Schneider does not seem particularly impressed. In fact, he does not seem anything at all. I poke him again with my finger, then point to a curve where mist from a swamp creeps over the road. Red-winged blackbirds perch on the cattails, chattering.

"Say a truck rounds that turn in our lane. You can't stop, he can't stop. Bam!" I slap my hands together and he flinches.

"Where does that leave us? Dear faithful departed. Eternal rest grant unto us.

"Or say you don't die. You're a vegetable for the next forty years. What about that? Is it an accident? Is there any such thing?"

Schneider squints ahead. "I don't see a truck."

I sigh. "That's not the point. There could be. Anytime."

"But there's not," he says softly, pulling on his St. Francis face again.

God, I hate being tolerated. I'd rather have a fight. Schneider shakes his head, weary.

I wasn't always like this. I used to be patient, long-suffering even. I don't feel like myself anymore. Or maybe it's that I've become too much of myself, that the mask has finally slipped. I say what I think. There's no time for tact and diplomacy. If people don't know what's on my mind now, they may not get a chance later.

"So what happened next," Schneider asks, humoring me.

I rap on the dashboard and shriek an imitation of Mrs. Moon's voice.

"WAKE UP," SHE HOWLED MONDAY MORNING, BANGING ON my door with her hard little fists. "Mass is at eight." It was seven-thirty.

"I'm awake," I pleaded.

"I won't have you going back to sleep on me. Open up."

I stumbled to the door and pulled it ajar. Before I saw her face I felt the heat of her body. Her complexion matched the streak in her hair.

"Are you all right?"

"All right?" she cried. "I been standing over a hot stove for the past hour."

"There's breakfast?" I hoped not. Back then I felt better adhering to church law.

"There'll be none of that anymore," she replied sharply. "Not until its proper time." Her heels hammered the floor as she marched back to the kitchen.

I sat on the edge of the bed, not daring to slip back under the covers. I stared dumbly toward the window, barely able to focus. Sunlight dappled the sheer curtains.

My clothes were thrown over the chair beside the bed. The room was a cell, really, spare and spiritual. Depressing is another word that applies, though a few years passed before I admitted it. Unger had furnished the room with one chair, the bed, and a simple crucifix. Everything needed repair. The bed sagged and the chair wobbled and Christ's nose was chipped. And still I found it cheerful, because I thought I wanted a simple life. I pulled on my cassock and hurried to church.

Eight sisters, one for each grade, were already herding school children into their pews. The nuns looked identical, their faces glistening from harsh soap and hard scrubbing. Peering out the sacristy door, I recognized only the superior, Sister Perpetua, who was at least six feet tall. She had collared me at the convent Sunday evening, explaining with odd intensity that her patron suffered "the most cruel torments" before her martyrdom.

The snuffling mob whispered and poked and bickered in the center aisle. Sister Perpetua pulled a bony hand from under her robes, raised it, and snapped her fingers, intending that they all genuflect at once. Some fell on their right knee, others on their left. A goodly number did nothing at all. Perpetua snapped her fingers again, and the bobbing in the aisle slowly ceased.

A morning breeze swept in from under the elms. The children's faces shone in the early light. An altar boy rang a bell and the mass began.

In the choir loft a nun assaulted the organ. Hosannah! The youngest girls warbled from key to key while the older boys' voices cracked. It was heaven to me, the sound of angels,

except that these angels walked out of their fathers' barns
with manure caked to their shoes and wiped their noses on
their sleeves.

"Oh Holy Ghost, Creator blest," they sang. Two dozen of
the town's oldest women croaked along in the side pews. A
mildewed God looking down from the leaking ceiling where
He presided, up to his elbows in cherubs. I set wafers on the
pink tongues, I listened to the organ groan. I blessed the
silence that came too soon.

Perpetua rose in the final pew, lifting that gray hand again.
Two hundred prisoners dragged themselves off to the last
day of school.

BECAUSE MRS. MOON POSTPONED BREAKFAST DID NOT MEAN
she neglected it. In the dining room pancakes ran with rivers
of syrup. Bacon was stacked like firewood. She carried in
bowls of potatoes and peaches and a platter of rolls, enough
to feed all the apostles and most of the saints.

"Eat!" she demanded, and so I ate. I ate until my eyes felt
like egg yolks floating in my pale face. Each time I heard
Mrs. Moon's feet rap against the floorboards I hoisted my
fork again.

"Pie," she cried.

"Later? Could I have it later?"

"So you're not hungry?" she said, her suspicions con-
firmed. I didn't recognize the meal for the elaborate bribe
that it was. She jerked away my plate, and stormed into the
kitchen. I was left with my fork still in hand, staring at the
skin-and-bones Christ who hung on the wall.

When she returned I sat upright, guilty though not sure
why. She polished the table, her dishrag orbiting invisible
stains. Her actions for the first time seemed purposeless, as if
she were uncertain of herself.

"I need you to help me, Father," she said finally, overcom-
ing her pride. She dropped the dishrag and wiped her hands
on her apron.

I wanted to help everyone and was at the age where I was sure I could. "I'll try," I said, falsely modest.

"My husband." She looked out the window. "We buried him out at the country church when we had the farm. The church is shut five years and the cemetery is full of weeds. He wasn't no saint. I don't say he deserves better. But when it comes my time I don't want to be laying in the ground alone."

"Well, this—" I said. She cut me off.

"I got two lots behind the church here in St. Jude, one for me and one for him. Our undertaker, Smit, he says he run into a spell where nobody's dying. He got time to do the digging. I need you to bless the grave."

"Why did you wait so long?"

"I wanted it done by a believer. What good's a prayer from a priest who ain't?" She gave her dishrag a sharp twist.

"What was wrong with Father Unger?"

Color rose to her already flushed cheeks. "He . . ." she began, then stopped herself. "I was thinking we could do it after breakfast," she said.

"Today?"

"What else are you doing?" she said quickly. "Smit and me and my daughter will be waiting out by the church door at ten."

"Thanks," I replied, grateful for the world's misery. Without it, who'd need me?

SHE WAITED THERE AS SHE PROMISED, WEARING A DARK BLUE dress and black gloves. Her face was hidden by a veil, as if her husband had died that week. Mrs. Moon, for all her rough edges, had a dramatic streak. She believed in doing things by the book, at least when the book suited her purposes. Since this was more or less a funeral, Mrs. Moon was in mourning.

A woman who could only be Mrs. Moon's daughter stood beside her. Lucky daughter; though the two resembled each other, the overall effect was not the same. Mrs. Moon was hard, gnomish. Her eyelids sagged and her skin was mottled and her long nose bulged at its tip. Her daughter's eyes were wide and green. Had she been less thick she might have been beautiful. She was a solid woman in a frivolous, lacy dress, and there was something heartbreaking in that. The dress was for a different woman, someone less firmly planted on the earth.

"This is Mary, my daughter," Mrs. Moon said. Mary nodded, not bothering to speak or smile.

"There's no sign of Smit," Mrs. Moon added. "Not that it's a surprise. He'll be late for his own funeral." She snorted. Her daughter sighed.

Mary looked down the road, not really watching for Smit so much as ignoring us. Mrs. Moon glared at her briefly, then pulled from her purse a mirror, of all things. She primped, adjusting her veil, patting her hair into place.

Birds gossiped in the trees. The wind lifted tendrils of red hair from Mary Moon's neck, blowing them across my face. Her skin was pale and lightly freckled, begging to be touched. There was no ring on her finger.

I asked her if she worked. Her answer surprised me, not for what she said but how she said it. She had inherited her mother's voice.

"At the Lakehouse," she blared, and clammed up again.

"What do you do?"

"I'm on my feet from five in the morning till four in the afternoon. I'm a cook is what I am. I spend all day in a tiny kitchen that's hot as hell." Her tone dared me to argue.

"We're not in the country anymore," her mother snapped. "You got a city job. You might as well get used to it."

"I'd rather be cleaning barns."

"You wouldn't know which end of the pitchfork to hold," Mrs. Moon said. A nervous silence fell on us again.

When I could, I glanced at Mary. She was like a plum left too long on a windowsill, heavy and ripe. She didn't seem the type to go unmarried, but then neither did she seem the type to tolerate fools, which thinned out the crop of suitors. But those wide hips were made for bearing children. And her breasts, what a broad, soft pillow for an infant's head. There was just the matter of her voice.

I couldn't bear the quiet. "You don't have a family?" I asked, just to stir things up.

Her mother's lips tightened. Mary studied me coolly and looked the other way. I saw the hearse turn a corner—sweet chariot!—and said, too quickly, "That must be Mr. Smit."

SMIT'S HEARSE WAS A BLACK MIRROR. I SAW MYSELF REFLECTED in the door panel, walleyed and melon-headed, a grim joke. Smit leaned out the window, cigarette smoke rising in a haze around his head. He tossed the butt on the street.

The undertaker introduced himself sadly, a professional conceit. "We'll be seeing each other more often than we like, I'm afraid," he said. "It ain't happy work."

"There's a better world waiting," I said. These days I'm not so sure and I'm in no rush to find out. Smit knew enough not to argue.

He nodded at his companion. "I'll be helping Alois here do the digging," Smit said. "This is Alois Pentz."

Pentz reached across Smit, extending a huge hand. It was tough, a workingman's tool. "Alois," he said.

"Always," I said, pronouncing it the way he did. I laughed alone.

Pentz looked at me, baffled. "Ja," he said. He had a strong jaw and a thick head of brown hair that fell over his forehead. He looked like one more overfed farm boy, except for his eyes. Alois Pentz seemed half-asleep.

"We can't sit here all day," Mrs. Moon said. She and Mary were already in the car. I climbed in and Smit pulled away from the church with a jerk. A pair of shovels and a pick rattled on the floor.

Smit delivered an undertaker's tour as he drove, pointing out the window with a tobacco-stained finger. "Schloess, the baker," he said. "Over there. His wife died last spring. Found her face down in a pile of flour."

"A coffin the size of a piano crate," Mrs. Moon said under her breath.

Smit almost laughed. "But a beautiful funeral, wouldn't you say, Mrs. Moon?"

"Nothing like Hilger's. That was a funeral."

"A beautiful service," Smit said reverently, most likely remembering the bill.

They went on like this past the city limits, into the countryside where there was nothing but fields and woods and a few scattered farmsteads. Smit peered off toward the horizon, pointing to a distant house. "Shinders," he said. "The old woman passed on three years ago, from—what was it, Mrs. Moon . . . ?"

"Brain cancer," she said, full of phony grief.

"Right, and the son took over the place and got married in, let's see . . ."

"Six months back. December," Mrs. Moon said, this time with relish.

". . . and from what I hear," said Smit, "the wife is expecting any day now." He lit another cigarette.

Mrs. Moon snorted again with joy. I would not call her evil, not exactly, but she got more pleasure from others' misery than anyone I've known.

At the top of a long hill Alois Pentz lurched forward and stuck his thick arm out the window. He pointed to a farm that looked abandoned. "My place," he declared.

The seasons had stripped away the paint, bleaching the wood gray. Most of the barn's roof had collapsed. A donkey wandered through a pasture filled with rusted implements.

"That's quite a place," I said. Mrs. Moon clucked and shook her head.

I studied the cornfields, lining up the rows as we drove past. Mrs. Moon and Smit exhumed people I had never met. The Bruns, the Penkes; they could have afforded more, Mrs. Moon alleged. Smit shook his head sadly. Too true, Mrs. Moon, too true, he said. Mary stared out her window, ignoring us all.

Anyone could see she was unhappy. If you got close

enough I'm sure you could smell it on her, underneath the
cheap toilet water and the lingering smell of greasy food. But
Mary Moon's unhappiness was an essential part of her charm.
Just as any fool could see she was unhappy, any fool with a
shred of vanity thought, I could change that. Which may
have been true, if only Mary Moon had agreed that happiness
is preferable to unhappiness. Poor Unger's mistake—and not
his only one, God knows—was his failure to realize that. In a
certain sense Alois was smarter. He didn't want to change
her; he sought to change himself. Not a noble goal, and
certainly no better realized, but more practical. Alois deserves at least that much credit.

SMIT'S CAR FOLLOWED A PAIR OF DIRT TRACKS THAT LED TO
a clapboard chapel. It stood alone on a hill, in a field of
tangled weeds burned brown by the sun. The windows were
broken out. The steeple had been hit by lightning. Smit drove
up the hill and turned off the engine.

The wind replaced the motor's rattle. At first I heard
nothing and thanked God for the silence. The sound started
as a whisper, shifting in tone as I turned my head. The
wind on the open rise was ceaseless, demanding. I began
to hear murmurs, voices, and words that did not exist except
as an illusion. It was the wrong place for a church. I wanted
to leave.

The tools rattled on Alois Pentz's broad shoulder. Smit
pulled a short wood box from the hearse. "The grave is this
way," Mrs. Moon said. We followed her through the weeds,
around to the back of the church.

A few dozen tombstones stood on the overgrown hill. "It's
over here," Mrs. Moon said. She wandered among the graves,
lost. "I never thought I'd forget where I buried that man,"
she said to herself. Finally she dropped to her knees and
pushed aside the weeds. A small stone set flush with the sod
said "Ernst Moon" and nothing else.

"He was forty-seven," Mrs. Moon announced to no one in
particular.

"The prime of life." I thought I should say something.

"If he had a prime it was before we met."

"God judges," Smit said, his mourner's voice low and sad and cloying. He was bone thin, barely more than a skeleton himself. He hung his black coat over a tombstone and picked up the shovel, grunting as he pushed it into the dirt. In his hands even a shovel sounded sad.

Mary took her mother's arm and led her to a misshapen maple that stood off by itself. I watched the two men dig, waiting for Smit to tell me what to do.

"You might as well sit down," he said.

"You've got three tools," I argued. I hadn't learned that priests make most men nervous.

"I figure Mrs. Moon needs you." Smit turned back to his work.

I joined the women and felt weaker for it. We sat together in the shade and watched the two men dig, listening to their shovels scrape against the earth. Pentz worked at the head of the grave, Smit at the foot. Their heads bobbed and the dirt flew in a steady rhythm.

Mrs. Moon and her daughter sat silently. Each looked off in a different direction, unable to share even the same view. I couldn't stand the quiet. It was my job to comfort the grieving and there I sat, dumb as a stump. "What did he die of?" I asked Mrs. Moon.

"It wasn't work, I'll tell you that," she said. "He drank. He couldn't keep a job. The work that got done I did. I cooked, I cleaned, I did the wash. In the morning he swept out the bar. A job for a teenage boy. That's what he did."

"Let him rest, Ma," Mary said.

"Not after what I endured." Mrs. Moon's eyes narrowed into hard, little slits.

"You and him both," Mary said. Her eyes turned watery but she didn't cry.

I mumbled something about God's inscrutable plan. If either of them were comforted they kept it to themselves. Mrs. Moon pulled out a rosary and worked the beads, her lips moving as she prayed. Mary closed her eyes and let her head drop in the grass. Smit and Pentz stood in the hole they dug, working like a machine.

I watched the fat cumulus clouds blow across the sky, gray, purple, brilliant white. Mrs. Moon dropped the beads back in her purse. "I still want myself buried next to him," she said. "It's bad enough living alone."

SMIT'S MELANCHOLY VOICE ROSE FROM THE PIT, CALLING TO us. He and Alois stood in the grave, poking at fragments of wood with their shovels.

"I thought you might want to watch," Smit said from the bottom of the hole. A thin, blue vein pulsed on his pale temple. Alois Pentz worked his shovel carefully in the clay, never looking up.

He fell to his knees and started digging with his hands. Alois's back was a broad plain of flesh and muscle that nearly filled the hole. When he stood again, he pulled back a rotted shard of wood. A skull glared back at us.

"I forgot he had a mustache," Smit said absently. The few hairs that remained were clotted with dirt.

A half-dozen ribs poked out of the clay. A jumble of bones—his hands—had settled among the ribs and vertebrae. A black crucifix was mixed in with them.

Alois Pentz lifted it out of the dirt and handed it to Mrs. Moon.

"Should I keep it?" she asked me.

"You know better than I do."

She crossed herself, then turned the crucifix slowly in her hands, wiping away the dirt. She pulled a white kerchief from her purse and wrapped the crucifix, her fingers soiling the clean cotton. Smit and Pentz gathered the bones and dropped them in the box.

"I can't stand that sound," Mary said.

Mrs. Moon and I walked with her to the crest of the hill. Fences marked the land into neat rectangles. Crops divided the fields into parallel strips. The pastures were green, the fresh-mowed hay gold. Farmhouses nestled in the windbreaks.

"There ain't much left," Mrs. Moon said quietly.

"I can barely remember," Mary said. "I'm not sure what happened and what I made up.

"We went to the parades in town. He held me on his shoulders and I could feel the bass drum in my belly. That must have happened. I remember it so clear."

"I don't know," said Mrs. Moon. "I sure wasn't there to see it."

Smit fastened the lid on the wood box, his hammer ringing against the nails. Alois shoveled the dirt back into the hole and we walked to the hearse. I carried what little was left of Ernst Moon.

THE FIVE OF US STOOD AROUND A SMALL HOLE IN THE cemetery back in town. Ernst Moon's name was already carved in a block of granite that lay flat near the grave. Mrs. Moon left a place for her own name to be added later.

Alois Pentz leaned on his shovel, no sign that a single thought occupied his mind. In a way I envied him. Nothing was required of Alois except that he shovel the dirt and fill the grave. The tool was a toy in his hand. He swung one foot, watching the seed float from the dandelions he ruffled. The silence was my cue.

Ernst Moon, I thought, I don't have any idea who you were. Is it true you were a drunk? Did you bring your wife to grief? Did you poison the body God gave you? Why then do we remember you?

Because we fear for ourselves. Because in the end we will be indistinguishable from you. If we forget the least of us now, how much more will be forgotten later? How will they tell our bones from yours? Who will remember?

These days that's exactly what I'd say. I've turned judgmental, harsh in fact. Not very Christian, but there you have it. Yes, yes, I know: Judge not, lest ye, too, be judged. But what kind of advice is that, when every act represents a judgment?

"Dust to dust, ashes to ashes," I said over Ernst Moon's

remains. "That above all others is the rule of our lives. The same God that charts the flight of the sparrows watches as we commend to Him again the immortal soul of Ernst Moon. He lived among us as a friend, father, and husband, yet for as well as we thought we knew him we can never understand the peace that he had made with God. We pray for him and for ourselves that we meet again."

As I say, I was a puffed-up little fool.

I took a handful of dirt and scattered it on the box. They all muttered, "Amen." Smit walked off with Mrs. Moon and Mary. I wiped my hand against my black cassock. The soil stuck to my sweating palms.

Alois Pentz and I were left at the grave. I took the extra shovel and helped him cover Ernst Moon's bones. The weight of the dirt was satisfying in a way no words could be. Next time, there won't be enough for even a small box of bones. Next time there will be nothing left at all.

The sun hung just below the trees as we finished. Alois's skin, smudged with mud and sweat, seemed to glow. "I'll be going home," he said.

"You live there alone?"

"No, no," he said. The voice made no sense with the face. It was a singsong dialect somewhere between English and German. He sounded naive, unformed. "I got the chickens and cows. Then there's the donkey and the dog. There's always something going on."

"Family," I said. "I was thinking of family, Alois."

"I'm there alone. Poppa died eight years back and then my momma passed, too. It's just me now."

I told him I was sorry. His eyes were half-closed. The slightest grin tugged at his lips. Alois looked as he had all day—like a man about to remember a dream.

"I want you to come out and bless my new chicken coop," he said. He ran his foot over the grass and a cloud of dandelion seed rose again. "My daddy had his barn blessed. It lasted longer than he did."

"A chicken coop?" A blessing seemed extravagant.

"Ja, for chickens," Alois said.

I looked into those eyes again and decided that explaining myself might take longer than the blessing. "I'll be there Wednesday morning," I said. At least he was a believer.

"It'll be painted by then," he said, shouldering the tools. He walked off humming to himself.

"SCHNEIDER," I SAY, "LET ME TELL YOU SOMETHING ABOUT this business."

He does not even blink now. He watches the road, incapable of so much as a grunt. How age is cursed! I could teach the young twit so much! Yet he is certain the world is changed forever. The old man lives in the past and the past is gone—that's the thought that buzzes inside Schneider's head, like a fly in a dark, empty room.

"Small towns," I tell him, "everything you need to know drops on you like the rain. The rumors and gossip soak you through. There's no way to make it stop, no way to know what's true. If the town is quiet it's all the worse. The quieter it is the more people want to see it explode."

He yawns.

MRS. MOON WAITED FOR ME BEHIND THE SCREEN DOOR THAT led into her kitchen. Her mourning over, she had changed back into a faded cotton housedress and apron. She unlatched the door to let me in.

"Why do you hook the door?" I asked her.

"You never know what's loose," she said, latching it again behind me.

"Here?" I laughed.

She pretended not to hear. "What did Pentz say?" she asked, eager to suck me dry.

"He lives there alone."

"They're all dead but him."

"He wants me to bless a building."

"Hurry before it falls." She banged a pot into the pine cupboards that ran from the floor to the ceiling.

"Something new."

"I bet. The last one who had any sense there was the old man. Now there was a worker. That barn you saw today—there was no better barn in the county. Milk cows out in the pasture behind it. Corn off beyond that. Fruit trees around the house and wine in the cellar. If I'd had a husband like that . . ." She stroked her wiry hair, unable to flatten it against her head.

"And his wife was a bird, never healthy two days in a row. Alois was their only child. The man deserved better.

"It was Alois that found old Pentz. He saw the horses wandering in the corn, pulling the plow. They were headed off for the creek. He found him dragging in the dirt, the clothes rubbed off his body.

"That was a beautiful funeral," she said, caught up for a moment in the memory.

"Alois ran the place with his mother. I say she died of the work. I don't care what the rest of them say about it. That's all rubbish. She never lifted a hand while Pentz was alive. She and Alois, they had the place to themselves.

"Alois. Well, you seen him. His neighbors, they bought the fields from him when the bank wanted money. Alois was left with the house and the barn falling down around his ears. A wife, that would have helped. But who would put up with that?"

"With what?" I asked.

"You can't see?"

She folded her apron and hung it on a hook behind the door. "You worry and what good does it do," she said, with more satisfaction than anguish.

I WENT BACK TO MY ROOM THAT NIGHT AND SAT AT THE window. The curtains, smooth and white as bare skin, undulated in the warm night air.

I didn't sleep for hours. I saw the crucifix wrapped in Moon's dull bones and couldn't get it out of my head. The skeleton could have been anyone's. It could have been mine.

Then the curtains brushed against my cheek, soft and

warm and almost alive, like a finger run across my face. I praised God for creation and cursed the temptation it presented.

"WHERE'S THE TEMPTATION?" SCHNEIDER ASKS.

"What are you talking about?"

"Temptation. You were talking."

So I was. Sometimes I forget—the line between what is inside and outside of me gets blurred. I say what I think and think instead of talk. I should worry about it more than I do.

Temptation. So that's the subject. Well.

Schneider believes his generation invented sex; he can't imagine that all the flowers blooming now bloomed then. Mary Moon, I thought that night, now there is a fallow, fertile plot. She's no slip of a girl, not by a long shot. Her beauty is in her solidity. Her shape rises and falls as smoothly as the rolling hills. She has the voice of a crow, and that would take some getting used to. But she couldn't talk all the time.

"Watch the road," I say to Schneider, as though that answers his question.

LET ME SAY ONE MORE THING ABOUT THAT NIGHT. AFTER hours spent begging, pleading, and wheedling with sleep, my mind finally, mercifully, went blank. Far more suddenly I was jolted back to wakefulness again. Something was crawling on my legs. I turned on the light and pulled back the sheet. A dozen ticks, maybe more, had buried their heads in my skin. One had worked itself up to my scrotum and was feasting there. They came from the cemetery surely, riding the weeds, waiting for fresh, warm blood. I plucked the parasites one by one and crushed them on the floor.

TUESDAY

YOU CAN PRETEND A CHURCH RUNS ON GRACE OR DIVINE guidance or whatever you want to call it, but the truth is, it runs on money. This isn't just personal opinion. The pope himself would hem and haw and say the same. Of course, I come by this insight more naturally than his holiness. His father wasn't an accountant. Mine was born to the trade.

Dull man! His eyes lit up only when they settled on a column of figures. I think of him as dusted gray by pencil lead, eroded by a steady flow of numbers. He was pallid, slight, infinitely boring. Out of respect for my mother I believe he had hidden qualities. What were they? Don't ask me. She never managed to explain his appeal.

"There's no money in the priest business," my father said when I announced my vocation. Won't that be a relief, I thought, sick to death of his dinner-table lectures on debit-credit accounting. How could I guess I'd spend my life fretting over finances?

Something always needs money around a church. The boiler breaks; the nuns plead for new blackboards; the bishop wants clothes for some jungle tribe. The demands are endless. You can't step up production to increase revenue. All that's left is to squeeze the faithful a little harder. It's God's work, I used to tell myself, but to be honest I never needed much convincing. In the end I was my father's son. I slept better with money in the bank.

Father Unger, it seems, slept better with company. He managed to keep his vow of poverty, however, extending it to include the whole parish. I found the bad news in his ledgers, which were sandwiched between Augustine's *Confessions* and Aguinas's *Summa* high on a dusty shelf.

During the best of times Unger made his entries in a pinched hand. When the parish's cash reserves dwindled, Unger's numbers shrank, as though he believed an expense written small cost less. For the last three months he made no entries at all.

I added, I subtracted. I interpolated and extrapolated. Regardless of what I did, my eyes ached and my head hurt and the numbers came out the same. I felt a nervous itching in my bladder. I've always had a physical reaction—an allergy, almost—to debt. I look at a workman's bill and I have trouble breathing. When I add up the cost of maintaining a parish it's like rocks on my chest.

Think of it: just as surely as evil walks the earth, paint flakes off wood. Shingles rot. Rain finds a leak. The furnace needed coal and the floors needed varnish and the pantry needed food. Which was to say nothing of the school and the convent and the eight chubby nuns. Where was the money for that?

Responsibility smothered me. Add to it the communion wine and Mrs. Moon's breakfast and the early summer heat and you see how I fell asleep. When Mrs. Moon barged in my face was flat against the ledger. There was some pity in her face, I think, but mostly what registered was disgust.

"They're here about the wedding," she said.

"What wedding? Who's here?"

"Check your calendar. It's all written down."

I shifted the papers left on the desk and uncovered an appointment book.

"See?" Mrs. Moon crowed, pointing at the day. "Leon Wegner and Louise Thuen. They're here. The wedding's

Friday." I was still decoding Unger's scratching when Mrs. Moon ushered them in.

I HEARD LOUISE THUEN BEFORE I SAW HER. "THERE'S A lot we got to take care of," she said, bustling through the door. She perched on the edge of a chair and pulled a notebook from her bag. Her foot tapped the floor and her hand smoothed her hair. She licked the tip of her pencil, crossed her legs, polished her scuffed shoe with her fingertip.

The groom stood in the doorway. "Leon," she said. "Don't just stand there."

He was a gawking blonde in a chambray shirt buttoned at the collar. His face shone from shaving and his neck was nicked and bloody.

"Congratulations," I said. He nodded quickly and sat down, stretching his hands out on his thighs.

Louise glanced at him and pursed her lips. "I'm gonna have the bridesmaids in organza dresses," she said, "and they're gonna stand right here." She sketched it out for me in her notebook. When she leaned over the desk I smelled powder and sweat. She was not quite pretty, but her manner defied you to think she was not. Her nose had an odd hook, and her ears poked through her lank hair.

There was the organist and the flower girl and the ring bearer and the best man and the bouquet and a hundred other details that drifted straight past me. I looked at Leon. His attention had shifted to the ceiling.

"What will you do after the wedding?" I asked him.

His lips started to move. Before he could answer Louise broke in. "We're gonna live out at my parents and Leon'll work the farm with daddy," she said.

Leon uttered his first words since walking in the door. "I got three brothers, so my home place'll be chopped up pretty fine."

"My two sisters, they're already out of the house," Louise added. "When daddy retires we'll have the farm."

She scribbled in her notebook. Leon examined the mud on

his shoes. I imagined him on some cloudless day, walking the fields to clear them of rocks. The flies buzzed around his head as he kicked at the dirt that was not quite his dirt, knocking loose rocks that were not even his rocks. He threw them to the field's edge, and as they clattered he wondered if the pebbles mated in the ground, breeding new generations to curse him.

"Now Leon," her father would say, "when you're done in the field we got to start cleaning out that barn." And no matter how softly spoken, the words grated against him. Because beneath them all he heard a simple truth: This is not yours. You are not your own man.

At night he slept with his wife in the same room where she slept as a child. He knelt between her legs and the alarm carried throughout the household. Her mother and father strained to hear the chirp and squeak of the rocking bed. "Quiet," Louise would say, and Leon understood that not even the nights were his.

He lived for the day her parents died. He dreamed of it endlessly, not out of hatred so much as self-pity. He imagined them in their coffins, he heard the will being read. And even though he could picture it all—those scenes were more familiar to him than the back of his own hand—still he was nagged by doubt. Each day of servitude wore him down, changed him forever. By the time the land belonged to him, what would be left. Who would he be?

I sat at my desk, hands folded, trying to concentrate on what Louise said. She paused and looked at me, waiting for a response. I cleared my throat and shifted Unger's papers.

"Marriage, as you know, is a sacrament," I said, figuring it was time I played my part. "It bonds you together to Christ and sanctifies the, the, marriage act. Has Father Unger spoken to you about the, uh, physical companionship of marriage? And what that implies?"

I prayed that he had, or that they would be kind enough to lie about it. Leon grinned. I looked at Louise. Pinpoints of sweat stood on her upper lip. As she straightened in the chair her breasts pushed against her cotton blouse.

She blushed. "He gave us a pamphlet. We both been studying it."

"I got just one question," Leon said.

"We already took care of that," Louise said abruptly.

"Excellent," I replied. "Excellent."

Louise consulted her notes. "The wedding starts at seven. We're gonna need you here early for pictures. And we expect you at the dance afterward." She checked a half-dozen items off her list and rose to leave. Leon got up so quickly that he tipped the chair. It clattered on the floor.

"Leon," said Louise, shaking her head again and sighing. He grabbed the chair with one big hand and set it right.

SCHNEIDER, POOR BOY. I SAY THE WORD SEX AND HE FLINCHES. I want to draw him out. It seems to me he has a problem.

I bet he has no idea what he's missing. You can see it in his face, especially around the chin. The bone recedes. The skin is loose, almost hairless. He's running away from the world. I know the type.

I poke his thigh. "Ever interrupted your experience with celibacy, Schneider?"

Color creeps up past his collar and curls around his ears. He tries to ignore me, but I know I've hit the mark. I'm on a first-name basis with shame and guilt. I recognize them when I see them.

Her name was Irene Rubia, and her father married the widow who lived next door to my parents. The first time I saw her was the day of the wedding, the same day I turned fourteen. She stood in the yard, sullen, her blue dress ruffled by the wind. Her legs were long and her hair was blond. If her lips were too thin and her nose too thick I didn't notice at all.

She was uprooted, which I overheard my parents to say might be the best thing for her. I introduced her to my friends. I showed her the neighborhood. I led her to the ravine where I had built a treehouse in a red maple. I knew I wanted to be alone with her, though I wasn't sure exactly why. Irene knew.

We climbed up the tree on slats I had nailed into the rough bark. The leaves were dense, the color of clotted blood. In the heat of the day the tree was alive with birds waiting for dusk to hunt.

"You like it?" I said to Irene, nervous and proud. The light was dim. A creek trickled at the bottom of the ravine.

"It ain't nothing like home." She tried to pout but didn't have enough lip for it. "I had a boyfriend, you know. Older, out of school."

My imagination churned. "Uh," I said.

"I get so lonely. In this stupid house. I don't know nobody."

I put my hand on her shoulder, all sympathy. "Hold me," she said, and I lurched toward her, uncertain how to get a grip. She eased onto the plank floor, pulling me with her.

I kissed her, a dry peck, and settled on my back. Our elbows touched. Flecks of sky appeared through the leaves. I knew there ought to be something more. I was still considering my next move when Irene said, "Is that all?"

"Huh?" I said, buying time.

"Here," she said, impatient. She unbuttoned the bodice of her housedress.

I slid my hand over her breast and felt the nipple budding into my palm. I didn't know what I was doing, but I knew it wasn't right. Irene sighed. I was frozen in place. Her eyes snapped open again, and she said, "Well?"

The blank look on my face told her all she needed to know. "Okay," she said, rolling me on my back. She tugged at my belt and unbuttoned my pants. Her breast poked from the open dress.

She kneaded and squeezed but I stayed soft as bread dough. "Come on," she said. I wished she would stop. She took me into her mouth and worked over me until finally she rose to her knees and exclaimed, "Christ, I give up."

I won't say that's how I heard my calling, but it gave me the idea I wasn't so well suited for this world. From then on I avoided Irene and prayed that she'd keep mum.

*   *   *

AFTER LOUISE AND LEON LEFT I FUMBLED THROUGH UNGER'S
desk and found the usual junk—pencil stubs, paper clips, a
penknife, holy cards, stale cigarettes, a broken rosary. He'd
stashed his marriage manual in the lower right drawer.

The pamphlet was filled with the same old gibberish.
Marriage And The Church. Establishing A Home. Managing
Money. Then, finally, The Marriage Act, with a pair of ana-
tomical drawings and some threats concerning contraception.

The marriage act. In the seminary the words stirred waves
of desire that swamped whole lectures. A sheet twisted and
falling off the bed. Legs intertwined. A musky scent, a gasp
for breath. The marriage act.

I saw myself swimming far from shore, stripping off my
cassock and watching as it sank slowly to the bottom. Mary
Moon floated naked beside me, her red hair spread on the
water like a halo. Why not? Why is it a sin to enjoy the
things God has created? Augustine says only God is the
proper object of our love, but that seems to me a narrow
view of His generosity. Might He not as easily take offense
when we fail to enjoy the things He created? What decent
theology is built on denial instead of joy?

I tossed the pamphlet into the drawer. As I pushed it shut
I glimpsed a package pushed far back in the corner, nearly
hidden. I pulled it out and unwrapped it. Inside I found a
pair of condoms from a pharmacy back in the city.

Someone banged on the door. I threw the condoms back in
the drawer and closed it. "Yes?" I said.

Mrs. Moon opened the door. She held a feather duster like
a scepter. "So what do you think?" she said.

"What do you mean?"

"You didn't look at her belly?"

"Belly?"

"Louise," she cried.

"Why should I?"

"Everybody else is. Half of them bet she's pregnant."

"I don't believe it." Really, I wasn't so sure.

Her mean eyes gleamed. "We'll see who's right," she said.

After she left I pulled the package from Unger's desk again and simply held it, dreaming of the possibilities. I knew I should throw it away.

Impossible.

I TRIED TO MOVE UNGER'S DESK CLOSER TO THE WINDOW, but it wouldn't budge. Mrs. Moon, drawn by my impotent grunting, stood in the doorway with her arms crossed. "What do you think you're doing?" she asked.

"What do you think I'm doing?"

"Don't snap at me," she said. "Anyway, you can't move it."

"What's the difference?"

"It's bolted." She pointed to the legs. A bracket fastened each to the floor.

"Why on earth?"

"You never know," she said, as though that explained everything.

I gave up. The desk stayed in its dark corner, which was just as well. The cracked top was stained with ink, burned by forgotten cigarette butts. Light wouldn't have helped.

Later I came to view the desk as a prop that, incidentally, held up paper. If I banged on the top it resonated like a fine old piano. A rumbling commotion—almost a thunderclap—filled the room.

Say, for instance, some backslider thought he had cause to question the Almighty's existence. I thumped the desk with an open palm, and His wrath seemed to echo in my office.

The evidence is everywhere, I said. Babies are born, the sun shines, the trees grow, and the birds stay up in the air.

And the innocent babies die. The sun burns off the crops. The trees can kill you when they fall. That's what my hard cases answered. Besides, they said, the scientists, they explain all that.

And I banged on the desktop again.

The scientists, I said, they can break the universe down into its smallest parts. They can study the smallest part of the smallest cell and still not understand what breathed life into nothingness. If life oozed out of the muck, then where did the muck come from? What existed before the first stinking soul-less particle?

Thomas Aquinas would not have been impressed, but if I raised my voice to a certain volume and pounded the desk firmly enough, my fair-weather agnostics gave up without much fuss.

Thank God for that. The more I talk the less I believe. Rattling on about God's nature always made me queasy. The world outside my window was mystery enough.

All I knew was the gossip Mrs. Moon hissed into my ear. "See that one," she'd say. "Velner, the boiler man. The one with the limp. His leg was burned by steam and the muscles, they grew tight on the bone. He was dead drunk, you can count on that."

Or, leering, "Did you hear about the Steinbraun's baby? The most beautiful red hair. I wonder where he got that from?"

She offered me a catalogue of weakness, suspicion, and sin. When I listened to her I alternately feared that I would never know St. Jude's thousand souls or that I would know them as well as she did and be crippled by what I remembered. Her version of the town's history was all avarice and corruption, death and disease, drunkenness and infidelity. It crossed my mind to tell her about the package in Unger's drawer, but I was afraid of what she might say.

THAT AFTERNOON THE CHURCH WAS QUIET, FULL OF SHADows. The Madonna perched on the earth with a snake curled under her feet. A fat infant Jesus rested in Mary's arms, and the crucified Christ's head hung loose on her shoulder. Candles flickered on the side altars. The air was sweet with old incense. My footsteps echoed.

I know that plaster eyes don't see. I know there is no life in a statue. But in that light and that quiet no one would be so sure. The building itself seemed to live and breathe. Then I heard voices.

They seemed to come straight out of the floor. I found steps that led down.

The basement was a catacomb of limestone and dirt. The only light entered from dusty windows set high on the wall. An altar stood at the far end. Four boys knelt before it, butchering Latin they read from their tattered missals. Sister Perpetua grimaced as she paced behind them.

"*Agnus Dei, qui tolis pecata mundi,*" she said.

They jabbered a version of their own.

"Again, *Agnus Dei.* Correctly this time."

"Good afternoon, Sister," I said. The boys' heads pivoted in unison.

"We're trying to learn Latin," the nun said.

I told her I was looking over the church.

"You mean you ain't been showed around?" the shortest boy said. He had buckshot eyes that looked familiar.

Sister Perpetua cracked his head with a knuckle. "Ain't?" she said.

"Isn't."

"I don't recall that anyone asked your opinion, Gabe," she added.

An older boy laughed. Sister Perpetua cuffed him, too.

"That goes for you, too, Mike," she said.

"Why don't I take this pair, Sister." She looked at me dubiously.

"Behave," she said, eyeing each of them. "Then come back when you're finished and you'll stay until you learn the Agnus."

"Bitch," the taller boy muttered as he swaggered toward the steps.

They waited at the door. They both seemed on the verge of puberty, sprouting pimples, gangly, insolent, and full of misplaced passion. I regretted rescuing them from Perpetua. When I came close they shot ahead. "This way, Father," Gabe yelled. I followed them up the stairs.

Something in both of them nagged at me. I tried to remember if I had met them before.

"What's your last name, boys?" I asked when I caught up
with them.

"Moon," Gabe said.

"Yeah, Moon," Mike added, defensively.

"And your parents, then?"

They looked at me as though I had asked which way was
up. "Mary," Mike said. "Just her." They broke for another
set of stairs.

I don't say it made sense, but I felt cheated and a little
sick.

Gabe was already seated at the organ when I pushed open
the choir loft door. "They told you about this yet, Father?"
he said. He had inherited his grandmother's brassy voice. "A
note so low it can stop your heart."

I shook my head.

"I'm going to play the one right next to it."

Mike pumped the bellows, and Gabe brought down a
stubby finger on the keyboard. At first I heard nothing at all.
Then there was a buzz that hovered at the edge of perception—
a million bees in a distant field of clover, thunder in another
county. The sound grew, the single tone working its way
behind the pillars, echoing off itself, until it seemed that the
chandeliers would drop and the walls explode.

Gabe leapt from the organ while the note still rumbled.
They were gone.

I found them in the attic, leaning against the brick wall.
The windows were covered with generations of grime. The
light was flat and dead.

The arched ceiling rose into the attic, flanked by a catwalk
of raw planking. Gabe and Mike led me over the cracked
boards to a spot above the altar. They pointed up to the
rafters.

"That's where they found the old widow. Hanging straight
down from that beam," Gabe said.

"Who was it?" I asked, certain he was lying.

"I don't remember," said Gabe. "But everybody knows about it. It happened a long time ago." Mike nodded.

"You're sure about this?"

"We heard it about a million times," he said, petulant. "That's why they call this the widow's chapel. Why else would they call it that?"

Their grandmother's obsession with all that was soiled seemed bred in their bones. I wanted to get away.

"We'll go up to the steeple now," said Mike. This time we marched off slowly together, neither of them speaking.

Mike opened a door. A wooden ladder led up into the shadows. The boys climbed it like monkeys. I groped for a handrail that didn't exist.

I hate heights. My stomach starts to twitch and the soles of my feet sweat and I feel a perverse urge to jump, even though falling is what I fear. I gripped the ladder, looking straight ahead instead of down. My knees shook. I had taken no more than a few steps when Mike sprang the bell tower's trapdoor, and a shaft of light fell on me.

"Come on," Gabe yelled. They both peered down through the opening.

When I pulled myself up into the tower Gabe struck the black bell with his fist. "If somebody rang the bell right now we'd all go deaf," he said.

He led me to the bell tower shutters. The whole county stretched out below us.

There was the creamery, there was the ball park. There were the train tracks that curved around the lake. The water was a sheet of blue, the clouds shadows on its surface. Beyond the lake, fields of crops and freshly mowed hay. Green and blue, blue and gold, as far as I could see.

Mike's hand pointed out through the opening. "See that old barn?"

I looked over his shoulder and saw what looked like a shipwreck. "Alois Pentz's place?"

"You heard that story already?" Gabe asked.

"I don't know."

"About his mother," said Mike.

"He killed her," Gabe said. "Poison, that's what they say. He couldn't stand it no more, taking care of her. He's crazy, everybody says it."

Look at them, I thought. If their pimples were healed they could play angels. Their lips were pink, almost delicate, and their cheeks were still smooth. Except for their hard eyes and the ripe scent of pubescence, you might check their backs for wings.

"Would you want someone to make up that story about you?" I asked. They studied the pigeon droppings on the floor.

"It's not a story," Gabe grumbled.

"You better get back to study your Latin."

I followed them as far as the choir loft, listening to their feet drag down the basement steps.

The church was quiet again. I watched dust drift through patches of light. From the choir the altar was no larger than a thimble on a table. My voice, I thought, it must be no more than a murmur at this distance. Could anyone hear it at all?

MRS. MOON THREATENED ME WITH ANOTHER PIECE OF CAKE after supper. "A priest can't look like a starved rooster," she said.

"What about Father Unger," I protested. "He was worse than me."

She muttered something in German and let the kitchen door slam behind her.

I fled to the park, which was speared with trees so young they quivered in the slightest breeze. A blank-eyed marble doughboy rose above the branches. I took a bench beneath him, skimming the few dozen names carved in the statue's pedestal. Buesgeuns, Huckenpoeler, Havenmeier, Koebnick: boys sent off to kill their relatives.

A pigeon strutting on the soldier's helmet spotted me and squawked, outraged. I saw Ernst Moon's name carved there among the others.

No one had told me he was a soldier. I tried to picture him

in the doughboy's uniform. All I could see were the bones that rattled in the undertaker's box. For me, Moon had no flesh. He was a skeleton and a crucifix and a few rotted boards. He was not even a memory.

A CAR STOPPED AND ITS DRIVER EMERGED BLINKING IN THE twilight, a bird freshly hatched. His nose was a fleshy beak, his legs spindly, his skull a smooth shell. He groped across the park as though it were already dark. He didn't recognize me until he was nearly in my lap.

"Kropp, Father," he bellowed. "Herbert Kropp. The entire family, all of us, all Catholics."

Mrs. Moon, I realized, had sketched his family history that afternoon as Kropp's wife walked by trailing a mob of offspring. "The sheriff's wife. Kropp," she whispered. "The man won't let her alone. Ten children. She's lucky if the next baby don't kill her." In the flesh Kropp did not seem so deadly a lover.

"Hard at work is what I hear," he said, "Replanting poor Ernst."

"I found his name here on the statue." I felt undernourished beside Kropp. He was not really taller, but he seemed to occupy much more space.

"Tattoo? What?" The sheriff turned a drooping ear toward me and stared from the corner of one eye.

"Moon. Here," I shouted. "On the statue."

"Moon!" Kropp blared. "What do you want to know?"

I shrugged. He seemed disappointed.

"Signed up with him for the war. Took the train together to Texas. For training. Sat next to me the whole time. Shouldn't never've left town. Moon, I mean.

"Woke up during the night. Flat. Corn everywhere. Iowa. Moon was wide awake. Had a pencil and paper in his hand." Kropp's ears twitched, waiting for me to say something.

"What did he write?"

"St. Jude, St. Jude, St. Jude, St. Jude. Over and over again. Covered the sheet."

Kropp ran his fingers over the names carved in the rock. "Should've stayed right here. Moon."

"Did you see him again before he came back?"

"You bet it's a fact."

"What?" I said.

A bramble of gray hair grew from his ears. "When he got home. He was lost. Nothing made sense. He had the disability. Lungs burned. From the gas. But you can't live on that. Couldn't keep the farm. Moved to town. He didn't know nothing but farming. Hires on as a salesman. Only job he could find. Rocks got more gab. Books door to door. German history. Bibles in three languages.

"Friday night." Kropp's clouded blue eyes slipped in and out of focus. "All the farmers come in. Women go shopping. Men in the bars. Town full of yammering people. Moon works the streets, selling his books. Nobody wanted to hear it. German history after the war? Most of them, they can't read anyway. Peddled books all summer, through the fall. Jesus Christ wouldn't have bought no Bible from Moon. The man had no heart for it, not for begging his friends. For being told no.

"Did their kids need Bibles? Bibles?!" Kropp's voice sailed through the trees and caromed off the church wall.

"Come ten o'clock Moon went for a drink. Stepped into the bar, forgot about work. Everybody's his friend. But he wasn't making no money. By fall, he brings the books along with him. Selling Bibles in a bar. By winter he don't have so many friends. Who wanted to hear it? Sunday, sure. You know what I mean. But Friday in a bar?

"So why didn't he quit?" Kropp asked.

"I never knew him," I said.

"What?" Kropp shouted. "Of course you didn't know him."

"Dead of winter. Friday night. Bars closed. Snow. Streets white. Cold enough to freeze your snot. Walking home and I see Moon. Sitting in the road. Drunk. Book in his lap. Tearing the pages. Throwing the pieces up in the air. No gloves. Hands stiff. Paper mixed in with the snow. Piled around him. Blowing away. Tears frozen to his face.

" 'Moon,' I tell him. 'What the hell.'

" 'It ain't what we left,' he tells me.

" 'This ain't no different at all,' I say. Because it wasn't, not then. I loaded him up. Took him back home to Mrs. Moon. Didn't see him again for months. Come spring he spent all the time with the girl. Mary. Spent his days here in the park. Pushing her on the swing. Catching her off the slide. Told him I could drive him around. Help him find work. Said no, his eyes were opened now. He didn't want that. He sat on a bench, in the sun, watching his girl. 'She'll be gone before I know she's here,' he said. 'I work every day and I die and she moves away and what do I know about her or about anything that's mine?'

" 'But you got to eat,' I tell him.

"And he says, 'My wife can't stop working. She'll work no matter what.'

"The girl," Kropp said, "she was pulling his hair. Yanking at his ears. Laughing. 'There ain't enough time to work,' he said. Girl ran off to the swing again. I walked back to the station."

Kropp stood with his eyes closed, quiet as the trees. "There must have been something he could do," I said.

He pretended to have heard. He scratched his ear, then shook himself and roared, "Gotta get to work."

I sat in the park until the moon rose, watching the bats sweep down from the church steeple.

WEDNESDAY

"HOW CAN YOU REMEMBER ALL THIS?" SCHNEIDER ASKS. IT
sounds more like a complaint than a question.

"I broke my hip. Not my brain."

"But . . ."

"Feel my skin," I say, holding out my forearm. Schneider
puts on an expression I've seen a lot of lately, one that raises
the question of senility without actually uttering the word.
He touches my arm but just barely. He's afraid old age is
contagious.

"So," I ask him, "remind you of anything?"

Silence.

"Like paper, right? Like the life's already out of it?"

Schneider's eyes are glued to the road.

"Now feel the muscle." He doesn't make a move. "Might
as well be wood. I get stiffer each year. My fingers get colder
each week.

"But I remember. I remember what happened fifty years
ago. It could be yesterday. I see their faces. I smell the sweat
and the dirt."

In fact, even these memories are moth-eaten. I know there
are holes, but I can't remember what used to fill them.

"Uh," Schneider says, clever as a rock.

"What else," I ask, "what else is left?"

I can't always fight off self-pity. Give me an audience and I'm shameless.

A PARENT LEAVES BEHIND CHILDREN AND I LEAVE SCHNEIDER. Not one chromosome of mine swims in his blood. His principal emotion on my passing will doubtless be relief. All the same, he's the only heir I have. To him I will my good advice.

I look at him and I see a pencil-necked bird crying from his nest, telling the world how to live. In short, I see myself when I arrived in St. Jude.

There I unloaded my suitcase and I filled it with rocks. I discovered the burden each generation carries and was horrified by its weight. Diseases diminished my flock, leaving the rest of us behind, abandoned. Glands I had never heard of failed to secrete hormones whose names I can't remember. Nerves I never knew existed came undone. Scream at the heavens for an answer and the clouds float by unperturbed.

We comforted ourselves as best we could. The town's houses filled with children and the town's bars filled with drunks. The melancholic spent days and months and years staring at a bobber. Fishing, they said. I recorded their names in the parish list, marking the dates of their baptisms, communions, marriages, and deaths.

Those pitiful volumes rest in the church basement, rotting, no doubt, and covered with dust. Not that it matters. I can't pretend the facts make much difference anymore.

"Where was I?" I ask Schneider.

"The chicken coop," he says. "What about Dentz's chicken coop?"

"Pentz. Alois Pentz!" Does the boy remember his own name?

"Oh, yeah," Schneider mumbles, glancing at the black plastic watch strapped to his wrist.

"YOU GOT SOME ANGELS TO CARRY YOU THERE?" MRS. MOON said. She dropped a ball of bread dough on the kitchen table.

I hadn't worked out the details of my trip.

She strangled the dough. "Try the shed," she said. "The bicycle should still be there. Not that what's-his-name ever used it."

"What's-his-name? Father Unger?"

"Ach," she answered.

Heat rose in waves from the wet grass. The leaves hung limp. My shoes got soaked in the short walk to the shed. I opened the door and it creaked, I breathed the dead air and nearly choked. The only light came through the door.

I clutched the doorpost, waiting for my eyes to adjust. Plaster faces looked out of the corners. Wise men, two shepherds, Joseph, The Virgin Mary, some barnyard animals, and a camel, all of them wide-eyed, exultant. A pair of seraphim hung from a rafter, trumpets at their lips.

The bicycle was in the corner, behind the Virgin. I rolled Unger's bicycle into the light. Closing the door, I heard a groan. The hinges, I told myself. I've got to get them oiled.

OUTSIDE HIS STORE, ART LIEBER MOVED IN SLOW MOTION, stacking vegetable crates under the awnings. "His wife ain't exactly faithful," Mrs. Moon had informed me merrily the day before.

Lieber's shirt clung to his back like wilted lettuce. He dropped a box of asparagus when he saw me peddling past and turned toward the street.

"Sunday is the baptism, ja, Father?" he called. I stopped the bike.

Sweat ran off his bald head. Lieber's features were broad, except for the tiny eyes that seemed buried in his face. The apron stretched over his bulging middle was stained with blood. He spoke with a Germanic accent—the whole town did. They all sounded a little thickheaded.

"You have a baby?"

"Eight pounds, fourteen ounces of baby, ja. Skin like, like . . ." He closed his eyes to think. "Like fresh veal."

Leiber seemed offended, as though I doubted his cantaloupes were ripe.

"And you have a name?"

"Dolores Elaine. A beautiful baby. A beautiful name."

"Then Sunday at eleven," I said, starting to push away.

"Wait," Lieber shouted. "Today without a hat your brains bake." He ran into his store and reappeared with a straw farmer's fedora. "A present," he said, "so that Sunday you're in your right mind. To a crazy priest God won't listen."

"Then the world's in trouble."

"Ja," Lieber said sadly.

I pulled the hat low on my head, humoring him, and gave the bike a push. From the chin up I was a farmer, from the neck down a comedian. The bike was too small. My feet dwarfed the pedals, and my knees chopped at the air. The bike rattled and squeaked. Lieber watched me from the middle of the road and waved.

I coasted down the hill that led out of town, past the swamp at the lake's edge. The smell of decay hung in the air. Frogs, insects, reeds, algae: all died, rotted, and settled into the muck. They became the muck, and only the swamp gas remained to prove they once lived.

That odor is still stuck in my nose, stronger now than ever before. The sulphurous farting of thirty old men fills our day room with the same stink. Back then I breathed deep and imagined that anyone who knew the smell understood God's scheme. Each year new reeds grew out of the ooze, fertilized by the decay of what came before. Who could smell it and see it and not be cheered? I coasted down the road with the wind rushing around my ears, howling with joy at the symmetry of this plan and absolutely blind to the grief in it.

The road leveled, the wind died. I pedaled through fields of corn and sorghum, gravel crackling under the tires. There was a hill. Sweat soaked my collar and stung my eyes. If I listen closely I can still hear the sounds—the rattling chain, my gasping breath, the flies buzzing around my head. The air was wet and heavy. Everywhere I looked there was green.

Trees and corn and pasture grass, everything thriving in the fertile heat.

Then I heard a scream.

I stopped the bike. Quiet. There it was again, high and piercing. I struggled through the tall grass. The ground fell away at the roadside, dropping into a steep ravine filled with brush and trees. A stream at the bottom was dammed with logs and rocks. Gabe Moon stood on a tree limb over the pool.

He was naked, his skin sinewy and white except for a few strands of pubic hair. His legs quivered and his muscles tensed as he tried to keep his balance. He was beautiful in a way I'm reluctant to describe. A gang of boys treaded water below him.

"You gonna jump or what?" someone yelled.

"I'm picking my spot," Gabe replied. He edged further out on the limb. The leaves around him trembled.

"You been picking a spot forever. Go on and jump."

His brother Mike grabbed a clump of mud from the bank and threw it. Gabe teetered as it hit his chest. I held my breath, waiting for him to fall. He grabbed at a branch and steadied himself.

Gabe smeared the mud around his nipples, between his legs. "I'm gonna piss on your head, Mike," he yelled. With one muddy hand he aimed a stream that splashed down into the pool. Mike dove and surfaced out of range. Another ball of mud splattered against Gabe's thigh.

He raised his hands above his head, wobbled on the branch and jumped. The leaves shook. Spray glittered in the shadows.

The tree limb was still. The water smoothed itself. Then the body rose from the dark water, limbs spread and face down. Gabe didn't move.

"Jesus," someone said. Mike reached him first. He raised Gabe's head from the water and yelled, "Come on, help drag him out!"

Gabe's hands darted around Mike's neck. He sprayed a mouthful of water in his brother's face. "Asshole," he yelled.

He laughed, a crazy cackle. I thought his black eyes picked me out of the bushes before he dove again.

The boys jumped after him, thrashing at the water. When Gabe came up they hauled him to the green bank, their naked bodies writhing in the weeds and mud.

They pinned Gabe and smeared him with muck from the stream's edge, their arms and legs a tangle. The boy lay spread-eagled, laughing hysterically. Their screams followed me to the top of the sunstruck hill.

BEFORE I SAW ALOIS'S HOUSE I HEARD HIS DONKEY. THE OLD animal bared his yellow teeth and wheezed an indictment against everything that existed.

I wished I spoke that language when I counted up the collection plates, for instance, or buried a baby, or opened the confessional door and sat down to another three hours of tedium. Let us bray.

Bless me Father for I have sinned, they said, year after year. I have lied and stolen. I've beaten my kids. I had impure thoughts. That's it, except maybe I drank too much. Isn't that enough? What more do you need to know? It's not the truth you want, now, is it? I wouldn't recognize it. I wouldn't know it if it banged on the door and introduced itself. So how can I mumble the words to describe it? Let's just say I lied and swore and drank too much and leave it at that. I did it this month and I'll do it next, but I'm sorry for all my sins, especially for those too hideous to confess, even here in the darkness, even to a faceless voice. There are some words I just can't say, words that describe the things I beg and wheedle and threaten to get. I see young girls in my dreams, Father, not more than my daughter's age. I don't want my wife the normal way anymore, I want to turn her on her stomach and, well . . . I wake up cringing, humiliated. Father, I lie and I swear and I drink too much. What more do you need to hear? Give me my penance and my blessing and let me out.

How I could have stretched my neck and howled into the

darkness! Send me a new sin, Jesus, one I've never heard before, one that gets stuck in their throats! Deliver me the truth! Please, please, please, show me something new under the sun!

The animal trumpeted again when I turned onto the rutted path that led to Alois's farm. I pedaled quickly, dodging the muddy puddles.

The pasture fence sagged to the ground beside the road. A field of stunted corn was filled with weeds. Alois, I thought, must trust the Lord to provide. He's not doing much to take care of himself.

A dog roused itself near the ruined barn, pricking its ears and sniffing at the air. It was black, a type of mongrel Labrador. The dog cocked its head as though to think. I froze.

The dog's legs stiffened. Its hackles rose. A growl rattled in its throat as it lifted its lips over long, yellow teeth. Then it folded its ears beside its skull and charged at full speed. Five feet from my bike the dog hurled itself through the air, foam trailing from its gums. Its incisors snapped together around the front tire. The dog pulled the bike out from under me and shook it back and forth.

"Cupcake! Cupcake!" Alois shouted. He streaked down the path, his boots pounding at the dust.

The dog curled its tail between its legs. It looked up mournfully, sighed, and loosed its grip on the tire, then slunk to the side of the road and rolled on its back.

Alois kicked the dog, catching it under the ribs and lifting it off the road. It rolled into the ditch, whimpering. I was stunned.

"Damn," he said. "Damn."

His face was set in the same expression he wore at the graveyard. He looked like a sleepwalker, someone who saw the world in a haze.

He lifted an arm to brush back his hair and the muscles jumped under his skin. He was heavy, powerful. He frightened me, the way a child with a gun might. He seemed unaware of his strength.

"Cupcake gets excited," he said. "He don't really mean nothing by it." The dog lay in the ditch, wheezing for air.

"That's what I thought," I said. I looked for a scar or dent on Alois's head that might explain him. Nothing. He turned to me and smiled.

"You want to take your bike?" Alois said. It lay twisted like a corpse in the driveway. When I bent to pick it up the dog growled.

"Let's forget about the damn bike," he said, irritation finally edging into his voice. "Let's get that building blessed." He steered me by the elbow toward the barn. The dog limped behind us.

The barnyard was bare of grass, the ground worn down into fine gray dust. A windmill creaked on an island of weeds, its blades turned by a breeze that never reached the ground. There was a corncrib, the barn, a low shed. Thin veins of red paint remained in the grain of the weathered wood. The buildings leaned out of kilter, collapsing from age and neglect. I didn't see anything newly built.

"What about that chicken house?" I asked, uneasy.

"Here," he said. "Right here." We turned a corner and arrived behind the barn. A rough lean-to was tacked onto its wall. I started to laugh but caught myself. I tried to imagine a suitable prayer.

Dear God, I thought, *send no rain, for this roof won't stop it. Lord Jesus, send neither wind nor driven snow, for these walls are a sieve. Give these chickens the good health they'll need. Look at brother Pentz's handiwork and understand that he trusts utterly in Your mercy, for he has done next to nothing to protect himself against Your indifference. Oh Lord, who hates the right angle, look kindly on Alois Pentz's labors, for he has longed to please You.*

"Seems like it's a little out of square, Alois," I said. "Will your chickens be safe in there?"

"My saw twisted on me right after I started. I just tried to match boards up as best I could. But it's solid, don't worry about that." He pushed at a corner with his huge hand. The building swayed. "No chicken's gonna push that hard," he said.

"What about the gaps in the wall? What about winter?"

"I figure by then I'll pull some more boards from the barn and nail them up."

"All right," I said. "All right. Let us pray."

I read a windy blessing, sprinkled some holy water, and said amen.

"Amen," Alois muttered, crossing himself. His donkey brayed, and the cows bellowed in the pasture. A hen charged past us, then a rooster, then the dog. Alois sighed.

"I planned on you staying for lunch," he said.

I wanted to leave.

"We can catch some fish. I got my own lake back here. Come on."

Alois headed off across the barnyard, conducting a tour as he pulled me toward his lake. Milk cows, goats, ducks! Yes! He had them! His thick arms shot out, pointing at tumble-down pens and sickly livestock, proud as Noah after the Flood.

"Father," he said, stopping to put his hand on my shoulder, "it's good to hear another voice out here."

His hand was warm, almost feverish. I nodded.

"I get lonely," he said. "In the day there's the animals making all their noise. But at night it's so quiet. I can't stay in the house. I hear the blood inside my head. I go out in the yard and look at the stars. So many stars and so much black, I think I must be dead except for the blood hammering in my head. Then the animals grunt and the bugs make their noise, and I know I'm alive because how else could I hear it? But it ain't the same as a voice."

"Well," I said, nervous.

"Look at my pigs," he shouted. Up against the barn's rock foundation five pigs lay flat on their bellies in the mud. "We cut through the alfalfa and then you see the lake," he said. I followed his trail through the field.

Alois stopped at the crest of a small rise and raised an arm—Moses now, Moses in bib overalls pointing toward the promised land. The lake before us was sky blue, its surface rippled by the breath of wind that struggled through the heat. A red rowboat floated near shore under a willow's branches.

"I sold other parts of the farm. There was bad years. It was like cutting off my hands to do it. But I'll never sell this."

I followed him under the willow tree. Two cane fishing poles and a shovel leaned against the trunk. The boat was tethered to a cement-filled can.

"Stay here," he said. "I'll go dig us some worms." Alois grabbed the shovel and waded into the weeds along the shore. I lay in the grass beneath the tree. The light filtered through the leaves. I could have waited for days.

Alois returned without the shovel, clenching both hands into fists. "Look," he said, uncurling his fingers. Long pink-and-brown worms squirmed in the dirt he held. "Night-crawlers," he said, dropping them into his pocket.

He picked up the anchor and tugged on the rope. The boat glided against the grass bank. Alois gathered up the fishing poles and pushed us out from shore.

"We'll swim first and fish later," Alois said.

He rowed to the middle of the lake, his back knotted with muscles. "Throw the anchor," he said. I eased the can into the black water. Yards of rope slipped through my hands. I tried to watch the anchor, but all I saw was my own reflection.

"This here's the deepest part," Alois said. He yanked his boots off and stood up. With a shrug of his shoulders the overall straps slid over his arms. The faded denim fell to the boat bottom and Alois stood before me naked. He sprung over the side, slicing clean through the surface. I saw a white shadow deep in the water, vague, shimmering.

The sun beat down on my cassock and the black cloth doubled the heat. I felt dizzy, almost sick. And still I did not tear at my clothes. It seemed wrong—unpriestly, dimly sexual—to stand there naked under the sun, my pink organs drooping beside my pale, pale skin. Alois breached the surface and spouted a mouthful of water.

"My lake don't bite," he said, sinking back into the water. I stripped off the cassock and stood there, longing to hide myself in the water, but also reluctant to jump. As Alois rose again I hit the water with the grace of a falling tree.

The lake was a cool caress. I swam to the anchor rope and pulled myself down, further from the sun and the heat. The water squeezed in on me, blotting out the light. Cool and green, then cold and dark; the weeds crept up my thighs. Far up above the surface shone with a silver light. Alois was a silhouette, stroking the water idly beside the boat. It could have been a kite, flying at the end of the rope I held. I pulled myself down further still until I was embraced by the weeds. My feet touched the slime from which the weeds grew. The bottom was insubstantial, enveloping, black. Fish, weeds, insects; settling, rotting. The dead sediment closed around me. I jerked my feet from the muck and bolted back up the rope, desperate to fill my lungs.

Alois laughed. "Oh, I was sure the weeds got you. I thought they pulled you right down." He rolled onto his back and spit another stream of water up into the heat. I struggled back into the boat, eager for the sun again.

The boat's motion rocked me to sleep. When I awoke, Alois was leaning against the bow, his head resting on his bunched-up overalls, more innocent than Adam in his nakedness. His uncircumcised member sprouted from a few golden hairs and fell, tumescent, between his legs.

WE STUCK WORMS ON THE SHINING BRASS HOOKS AND PULLED fish out of the water, one after another. They flopped in a pail on the bottom of the boat, still bright and glistening, gulping at the air and finding too much of the thing they wanted. Their bellies were orange and their gills dipped in blue. It felt like blasphemy, killing them that way.

"Bluegills and pumpkin seeds," Alois said.

I didn't know what he was talking about.

"The fish." He nodded toward them and smiled vacantly. They rattled in the pail, covering themselves with dirt and rust. Finally Alois put down his pole, and said, "That's enough." He drew up the anchor, swirling it in the water to wash away the mud. The oars complained in the locks as he rowed back to shore.

We cleaned the fish beside the barn. Alois pulled them from the pail one by one, stunning them with the butt of his knife and cutting off their heads. Their coloring, already dulled by the mud and the sun, dimmed and went dead. I scraped the scales loose with a tablespoon. They glittered one last time as they flew through the air, then dried and turned gray in the dust.

I'LL SAY THIS MUCH FOR ALOIS: HE DIDN'T TEMPT HIS NEIGH-bors into covetousness. His house tilted northward, away from the sun, and its clapboard was weatherworn to a silvery sheen. The porch floorboards were loose, springy with structural rot. The dog had chewed away a large portion of the door. Inside things weren't much better.

Alois pulled out a chair for me and set to work over a grease-smeared wood stove. He shoved a handful of tinder into the firebox and blew on the ashes. A flame caught and glowed.

"I suppose you heard already," Alois said, almost accusingly. "Why I'm alone. I know what they say." Grease sputtered in a black pan.

"I don't know. What do you mean?" I doubt I was convincing.

"About my mother. It's not true, what they say." He floured the fish and dropped them into the lard.

I sat quietly.

"Let me tell you this," he said. "If you never watched anyone starting to die you'd say no, it don't happen so slow. It was like summer turning into fall. You don't notice the change in any one day, but then it's winter and the snow's up to your eyeballs and you don't know where the time went. You feel like you wasted all those days.

"Her foot turned stiff and she didn't say nothing. When I noticed she said it was arthritis most likely. Then it crept up her leg, then her face started to twitch. I told her I was taking her to the doctor, that she was going whether she liked it or not. We went all the way to the city, on the train, just like you came out.

"They took her blood and measured her heartbeat and pounded on her knee to make it jump. At the end of the day we waited in the doctor's office alone. He was talking to the other doctors. They're all in on this together, you know. I put my hand on her shoulder and we looked out the window. We couldn't see nothing but the sky. Big clouds floating by, big white clouds.

" 'Ain't they pretty, Alois,' she said. 'Ain't they just something?'

"The doctor came back in twisting his lip and he cleared his throat and said, 'We ain't smart enough. We ain't smart enough yet to know what to do for you.'

"But we're smart enough for all types of things I don't want, I thought. Why ain't we smart enough for this. I didn't say nothing. I knew they planned on just letting her die.

" 'It's in the brain,' he said. 'It's like the brain is fighting with the body and they ain't talking to each other anymore. There ain't nothing we can do.'

"On the way home she told me that Jesus never worked miracles except on those that believed. She was a believer, that's for sure." He eyed me quickly and turned back to the stove. I felt more nervous than mournful, the agent of an untrustworthy God.

"Well, there wasn't no miracle around here. She got stiffer and stiffer until she couldn't move at all. I didn't have time to farm and take care of her both. I sold off land each year so we could live. Even at the end, when she couldn't do nothing but sit in her chair and look out the window, she told me, 'Alois, God sent us a beautiful day. Look at the snow, how it sparkles in the trees.'

"She couldn't see and then she couldn't talk and then she was gone."

His face was crossed with that odd smile, despite what he said. A pillar of smoke rose from the pan behind him. "The fish," I said softly.

"Damn," he said, whirling around. He pulled them black from the pan. "Damn. Damn."

He put the charred fish on a white plate, along with bread and pickles. I scraped the white meat away from the black skin and tried not to think of the taste. It all was burned.

"I ought to get going," I said as soon as I could.

Alois ignored me. "I get sick of being alone," he said.

"I know," I told him, sure he would never be anything but. He was marked, anyone could see it. He was born to live and die alone. It was there in his face, clear to everyone but Alois himself. If you looked at him closely he seemed to be assembled from spare parts, none of them exactly matching. At first glance he seemed boyish, a lazy angel. But then if you studied him you saw the lines in his cheeks and a hardness in his lips. Instead of ignorance and sweetness you saw something else, something unsettling. He was unable to awaken to this world and understand what others took for granted. He was pitiful and fearful in equal measure. I wanted to get away.

"I think of Mary Moon," he said. "With those boys. They need a home."

"I don't know," I said quickly, hoping he would stop.

"And I want a wife. Someone to help. To talk to again. I been alone too long. I hear things."

"You've got to consider what she wants."

"Well, who does she think she's gonna get?" he said, not waiting for me to finish. "After what happened to her."

"I don't know," I said again. "What do you mean, what happened to her?"

"You can't tell me you didn't hear. They don't give nothing any peace in town. You heard."

"I don't know what you're talking about."

"Ah," he said, disgusted. He pushed his chair back and grabbed my plate. He turned and let the plates clatter in the sink. "All I'm saying is you could ask her what she wants. That ain't no life for a woman with kids, what she has." He spoke flatly, his back to me.

I told him I had to get back. A lie, a venial sin, no more

than that. Who's to say anything would have ended differently, even if I had stayed and told him the truth? How could I have claimed to know it?

Alois stood motionless at the sink. I let myself out.

The dog was down near the barn, rolling in fish innards. A chorus of insects sang in the grass. I pulled my bike from the ditch and stamped Lieber's hat back on my head. Looking back, I saw Alois standing in the farmyard, watching as I pushed the bike back to the road.

In the west a wall of clouds hung on the horizon, a purple shroud cut through by lightning. Thunder rumbled at the edge between hearing and imagination. The sun still shone, but now the faintest breeze stirred, delivering the vapor that comes before a storm.

THURSDAY

THE STORM PUSHED IN AT MIDNIGHT. THE CURTAINS FLAPPED, rain splashed on the floor. I stumbled across the room to pull the window shut, then fell back into bed. The storm moved directly overhead.

What a racket! Thunder that shook my intestines. Cold, blue lightning sizzling in the darkness. Wind wailing in the gutters, all but inhaling the young apple trees. A real storm, the way storms used to be.

Why has the weather grown so lily-livered?

Don't tell me the weather is still the weather. Believe me, it's not. Even a layman can tell the oomph is out of the thunder. It seems to me the sky is also less blue. The newspapers report that the ozone layer is thinning out and the earth is starting to cook. The enfeebled polar ice caps melt a bit each year. Species after species disappears. I'm certain the world is growing old, run down.

I could go on at some length. I believe there are reasons that go beyond simple science. But please, don't get me started. I can't go wobbling down every dark alley that presents itself. The storm came and went and the sun rose. For now let's just leave it at that.

At dawn my face was still pushed into the pillow. I didn't wake until Mrs. Moon screamed, "Breakfast!" I sat up and stared at the floor, barely able to remember where I was.

The room was stuffy and hot. The window was closed. The storm. Of course.

Back then I always slept like one of the dead. Now that I'm so much closer to achieving that state I hardly sleep at all. Tell me, where's the justice in that? I'd love to sleep so soundly again, to dream the way I used to dream. Big dreams with bright swirling colors, dreams like David's coat. Old Testament dreams with blood-spattered doorposts and dark, oiled girls. Song of Solomon dreams. These days—I swear this is true—my dreams are in black and white, like a silent movie. All I see are grizzled farmers wandering dusty fields. Sometimes as I struggle to fall asleep I hear voices singing the old songs—patriotic tunes and ballads and lullabies. Don't think it's any consolation. No matter what the song, it's out of tune. The first few nights this happened I looked out the window, expecting to see some drunken fool vocalizing in the street. Now I know nobody is there.

I wake up for a hundred different reasons. My gouty toe begins to ache, or some fossil down the hall starts yodeling, or my bladder fills and I need to get to the toilet pronto. The nurses say a man in my condition should be in Depends, another euphemism that has attached to me and my tottering brothers. A diaper by any other name remains a diaper. And diapers are where I draw the line, at least for now.

"Breakfast," Mrs. Moon screamed again, rattling the door this time.

"I'm up," I pleaded, shaking my clothes and stamping on the floor so she'd believe me. She snorted and marched down the hall.

As I entered the dining room she slammed a platter of eggs on the table. The sun hadn't risen above the trees, but Mrs. Moon was already steaming.

I knew I couldn't wake every morning to that murderous face. I took hold of her wrist, stopping her before she bolted to the kitchen again.

"What's wrong?" I asked. Maybe her grocery allowance was niggardly, maybe the plumbing was bad. I could set things right easily enough.

She shook my hand loose.

"You'd never understand."

A dozen replies occurred to me at once and all of them seemed wrong. "Well," I said.

Her anger collapsed. When she spoke again her voice still had a sharp edge, but she seemed to be pleading, desperate to explain. "What I been through in this place," she said. "You can't understand."

"I can try."

"Oh, ja." She managed an empty laugh. "You can try. Let me tell you and we'll see. Let's start with the farm.

"A house and a barn and the snow on the fields. And then the woods, like a black wall in the snow. Black and white and black and white, month after month, all winter long with the moon and the night and the wolves coming down out of the woods. Wolves howling on the hill on a winter night, waiting and watching. Can you believe that? That's how raw it was. The wind blowing across the fields, blowing in through the cracks, cutting right through the walls. Waking up with frost on the blankets. Can you understand that?"

Once started she spoke in torrents, one word pulling out the next in a breathless stream.

"When Ernst came back from the war I saw he wasn't good for no farming no more. He lost a lung, he lost part of his stomach. He wasn't a farmer no more. I tell you—I'm not ashamed—I tell you I thought, hallelujah, now we sell this place and slaughter the animals and move to town and live like people instead of farmers. We work for a wage and we don't care ever again when it rains and when it's dry. We don't care when the hail knocks everything back into the ground.

"We were gonna be done with it. Ernst works and Mary goes to school and I make a home. Can you understand? It was so simple. Ernst works. He wasn't a stupid man. He could read and write. He works. He finds a job and works. And I wake up without the smell of pigs in my nose and I never again hear another stupid cow or a grunting pig and I don't fight against the mud and the dogs and the dust that blows for miles.

"Ernst works. He was missing a lung, yes. But he could still breathe. He could be a clerk. Maybe a banker. Or work for the newspaper. Or even sell books, if that's what he wanted. But he came back and he was lost."

"Lost?" I asked. "He drank?" I remembered what the sheriff said.

"Drank?" She coughed out a hollow laugh again. "I worked. I paid for the house and the groceries. He pushed his baby on a swing and read his books in a bar. And even so it was better. I could forget the smell of pigs. I got Mary free from it. She didn't have to get stuck raising barefoot babies in the dirt and pulling on a cow's teat all her life and dusting the endless filth from her house. Dust that blows every day it's able, that comes straight through the windows and the walls and settles over everything, working into the chairs and the rugs and piling up in the corners until you believe if you cut yourself open mud will ooze out of your veins.

"I buried him out in the country from spite, to put him back into the dumb earth and let it eat him up. So someday he's blown with the dirt over this county and he's carried out in a dustpan and then he blows again into the hog pens. So he's trampled underfoot. If I could have tied him in a tree to rot, that's what I would have done, for all the years I spent there. Let him blow in the wind. Let him scatter across the roads. Let him be the dirt under some woman's fingernails, and let her curse him every day of her life."

She talked to herself, explaining her life as though she hoped, finally, to see the sense in it.

"When Mary found a husband it was a farmer. A farmer! Or a man who thought he ought to be a farmer because he read some books about it once. Full of plans about what to plant and where the orchard will go and where he'll set the bee boxes and what tractor he'll buy. Not knowing a thing about farming or anything else, except making children. That he does fine. She has two boys. Devils. Where does it come from, what's in them? They'd as soon lie as look at you.

They're never satisfied. Always into something. Where does it come from? From their father? From Ernst? They weren't good or bad. Just ignorant, lost on this earth. They didn't know which way to turn to save themselves. Where does it come from?

"I'm the only one in the family who wants more and better and easier. I'm the only one. And this—" she waved her hand around the room"—this is what it got me. Mary's husband couldn't even drink himself to death, that's the ambition he had. When the corn died and the cows went dry and the pigs never grew to more than runts and there was no money left, then he disappeared. On a winter night when there isn't a cloud in the sky, that's when he walks away from Mary and his boys and his farm and all his bad debts. He leaves them and he might as well be dead for what they hear from him. I carried them on my back in the end just like I carried Ernst. And even so that ain't the worst of it."

"Tell me everything," I said. "Get it off your chest." Nothing in my drowsy upbringing allowed me to understand what she was saying.

"Mary and that . . ." She paused, reconsidering.

"What?" I said, too eager.

Her pinpoint eyes bored into mine. I believe she recognized the perverse joy that registered there. I could guess what she meant, but I wanted to hear the words. She wouldn't give me the pleasure.

"I work," she said. "I wear my rosary to dust. What changes?"

"It doesn't sound to me like the devil's work, Mrs. Moon," I said, full of fake piety. "To me, I think . . ."

I lifted my head in time to see the kitchen door slam behind her.

THE GOSPEL FOR THE DAY SAID, "BLESSED ARE YE THAT WEEP now, for you shall laugh." Any laughing Mrs. Moon did was not on this earth, so maybe she laughs now in heaven, if there is one. It's easier to picture her spitting bile with

Lucifer than tittering with cherubs, but who knows? I'm not so sure of anything these days. I'm certain, as I say, that I smell melting butter every time I walk past her grave. What sort of sign is that?

That morning during mass Mrs. Moon was the image of devotion. She mumbled her prayers from a pew in the back of the church, her shoulders bent and her head hung low.

Dust that had swept over the dead and the newly born floated through the light. I muttered the Latin words, beyond hunger and pain and pleasure until the organ shuddered its final note. Then I looked up and wondered: Can the world still exist?

The doors swung open to the sun and fresh air. The noise of the town pushed its way inside. The parish nuns stood blinking in the doorway, habits flapping in the breeze. The votive candles flickered as the nuns slammed shut the door, startling the few old women who remained. They knelt in their pews long after silence settled over the church again. Lips trembling, they prayed for their dead husbands, for their dead children, for themselves. Mrs. Moon was there among them.

In my sleepless nights I still see her daughter's husband, hurrying across the frozen fields to a road barely visible in the moonlight. The sky is black and the fields are white and the moon shines, hard and silver. With each step he hears the snow screeching a single word of advice: *leave, leave, leave.* He marches away from everything he tried to build and all that reminds him of his failure, planning to stop only when he is nobody, a man on whom no one depends. The stars shine empty and cold and his breath freezes in his nostrils and he walks on and on, hoping that through the ignorance of others he would find himself born again.

Soon enough I wished I were him.

I LEFT THE RECTORY AND WALKED THROUGH TOWN, NO PAR-ticular destination in mind. I nodded to the people I passed, uttered a few words of nonsense here and there. Up the hill to the public school, down the hill to the feed mill, past the bank with its bright marble facade. The air was clean, washed by the storm.

Let me tell you how it is with me. My instinct is to talk my troubles away, to use words like shims, jamming them between me and my problems. In St. Jude there was no one I could trust. Of course, no one seemed to trust anyone else, so I was no worse off than any of my neighbors. But my poor brain spun. I worried over the Moons and Alois and Father Unger. Instead of talking I worried, grinding away my nerves in the process. All that helped was to walk.

I guarantee you that pushing a walker down a nursing home hallway is no substitute. It's all clattering metal and shaky little wheels and fear. If I fall again I'm a goner. Or worse, not gone, just a bag of bones on a hospital bed, turned once an hour by some condescending twerp. Bed sores, you know, they eat my kind alive. Now there's no relief in the walking I do. Most days my head seems ready to burst. Have I already mentioned that? Well, so what if I have? And what if it does? My head, I mean. Better I go with a bang than a drooling, mindless whimper. Protect me from the doctors who save the husk after the grain is gone.

I patrolled every corner of St. Jude—not much of an accomplishment, really. Walk a few blocks south, west, or east and soon enough you bump into a cornfield. Go north and there's the lake. In my own way I loved the place but not so much that I'll lie. The truth is this: The town was in miserable repair. Roofs cried for shingles. Gutters swung loose. Everything needed paint.

I sat on a bench outside the Lakehouse Hotel studying the buildings across the street. A place called Steiner's Tavern was boarded over, a victim of Prohibition. The jeweler next door did his business in a shop with a cracked window and sagging steps. It was the same all down the block, as if one day the merchants decided that, since the battle against decay could not be won, they would no longer fight it. I wondered if there was a sermon in it, something about spiritual maintenance.

A thick hand settled on my shoulder.

"The sun bakes out your brains again, ja, and I end up with an insane priest to baptize the baby. After I give you the hat." A smile spread across Lieber's thick features. "Come in," he said. "We get a glass of tea." He pushed me through the hotel's door.

A row of rocking chairs stood opposite the front desk, beside a polished stove. Some violets were busy dying on a table near the window. Lieber hurried me through a narrow door, down a dark hallway, and into a back room. Into, as it turned out, a bar.

"Two," Lieber said to the bartender, who wiped the surface with a rag and set down a pair of beers.

Lieber's eyebrows waggled as he lifted his glass. Foam stuck to the tip of his nose as he set it down again. "Drink!" he said, and I did. It wasn't the last law I'd break that week. Lieber laughed, satisfied. "One way or another," he said. "I save you for the baptism."

As my eyes adjusted to the dark I realized we were not alone. Three men sat at a back table, beckoning to Lieber. They were all moon-faced and big-bellied, a tribe of old monkeys all nodding and mumbling.

"Who are your friends?" I asked Leiber.

"Oh, ja. New blood we see so rarely that manners we forget. I introduce you." He steered me toward the table, beginning his introductions from halfway across the room.

"Our pharmacist and mayor, Albert Krank. Owner of the First National Bank, Fritz Fitz. And the farmer and tomorrow father of the bride, Wilbert Thuen."

Three meaty hands reached toward me. "Mary," Lieber said, "bring the starving priest something to eat."

Mary Moon appeared in a doorway behind the bar, her hair piled up and her neck glistening with sweat. Without a word she turned into the kitchen.

"So, Father," said Krank, "your mind isn't poisoned by Lieber. What do you think about the sign?"

"The sign? I don't . . ."

"Haven't heard? Perfect. We have a plan. . . ."

Lieber interrupted. "Perfectly good money to waste. Because the tourist business is over. They go now somewhere else."

"You know how pigheaded Lieber is," said Krank, inflating inside his druggist's smock. "Afraid to spend fifty cents to make five dollars. Anyone with brains knows. Tourists don't care where they go. One place is as good as the next. It's all in their heads. Tell me, what's wrong with this lake! Why is any other lake better?"

He seemed to expect an answer. I shrugged.

"I been thinking," Krank continued, "of a sign that reads, 'St. Jude. Where Profit and Pleasure Go Hand in Hand.' Or something like that. Down the road at Cologne they already got one."

"And a collection of gopher holes it is," said Lieber, slapping the table with his palm.

Fitz cleared his throat, slowly bubbling to life. "What's the bill on this one, Mayor?" he said.

"We got a deal."

"Ja, how much it costs?" Lieber retorted.

"With the land that Wilbert here is giving us it won't cost a penny more than, oh . . ."

"We wonder, Wilbert," Lieber said quickly, "why the land you donate."

Thuen fingered his hat, glancing at the mayor. "Krank tells me the city crew will fix my fence after the sign is in."

"Ach," said Lieber. "Closer we get now to the bottom of this. This is not no gift."

The banker rumbled again. "What did they get out of the sign by Cologne?"

"You can't measure it with a ruler," Krank said. "You know that. But you take into account that they got the county fair there, too, people see it and they think the town is . . ."

"Filled with junk and gypsies," Lieber said.

"Exciting!" the druggist shouted, pounding the table. The coffee spoons clattered on the saucers. For a moment everyone was quiet. "So what do you think, Father?" Krank asked.

"I agree with Mr. Fitz," I said, since he hadn't taken a side.

"What do I think?" Fitz asked, perplexed. "But isn't it true Wilbert here will have a son-in-law to help with his fence Saturday morning?" he said finally. "Why does he need the city crew?"

"And a grandson, a grandson, too, before long he'll have to help." Lieber grinned. Thuen rubbed at his callused hands.

"We'll see how much farm I have after the wedding. The girl invited the whole county."

At that Mary Moon came to the table with a platter of sausage and cheese. As she stooped to set it down her breast pressed against my shoulder. For a moment I smelled her scent—the smell of the kitchen, and under that sweat and damp cotton. She smiled not so innocently. Her hip brushed against my ribs. I don't necessarily believe it was an accident.

"SCHNEIDER," I SAY. "MY BLADDER. IT'S NOT THE HIN-denburg."

"The what?"

"Never mind," I snap. "Just stop somewhere."

Every new year finds me more childish. My bladder and bowels obsess me. Lately the skin has sunken around my eyes. They're wide as an infant's. I look dazzled by the world, an appearance that is not exactly correct.

"Where? The Burger King?" Schneider asks.

"Do I look like anyone you've ever seen at Burger King?"

"You want to go to there?" Schneider points at a place called Erma's Cafe. The building seems to have crashed in the gravel parking lot.

"Maybe it's owned by someone who lives within five hundred miles of here," I tell the boy. "They might serve food somebody in this county cooked." But what difference does that make to Schneider? He was probably delivered at a franchise hospital.

He sighs, which is Schneider's most frequent expression in

my company. He sighs like a martyr, annoying the hell out of me.

I teeter toward the door, clutching my walker for dear life. Last year I was footloose, then it was a four-pronged cane. Soon even the walker will be impossible, and I'll be sentenced to a wheelchair, no chance of parole. I heard a doctor say that because my circulation is so wretched—his word—my left leg may have to come off. Villains! They intend to bury me a piece at a time, chopping away until there's just enough left to put a hat on.

Each step now is torture. Everyone pretends this is therapy, that I'll walk again as well as I did. What nonsense. I'm on my way out, but I'm not going peacefully.

Schneider waits for me, pushing all the tiny buttons on his digital watch. He times everything: the drive, the Sunday mass. Most likely he measures his time on the toilet.

"Forty-six minutes since we left town," he announces merrily as I pull myself up the steps.

"Hold the door," I say, planting my walker on his foot.

Inside two cadavers sit at the only occupied table, sending up a haze of cigarette smoke that clouds the fluorescent lights. A bored waitress leans against the counter. "What'll it be," she asks, leering at Schneider.

"Two sweet rolls and coffee for each of us," I say. She pulls the rolls from a plastic bag and slaps them in a microwave. She winks.

"Coming right up."

Schneider smirks.

"What happened to Erma," I ask.

"I'm Erma. Bought the place with my divorce money and I tell you it's the best thing I ever got out of that fool."

Schneider, unable to control himself, laughs, spraying coffee across the counter. "What's wrong with him?" Erma says. I don't bother to answer.

Instead I shuffle to the toilet, where a steamed-up blonde is pictured on a vending machine that sells something called a french tickler. It takes forever to squeeze out a drop of urine with that tart looking down at me. In seven minutes, fifty-six-point-five seconds—Schneider's estimate—we are back on the road.

ON MY WAY TO THE TOILET, FULL OF LIEBER'S BEER, I CAME upon Mary Moon. She sat in the kitchen peeling carrots beside a boiling pot. Steam mixed with the sweat that beaded on her face. She ran a hand across her forehead.

"Busy?" I said.

"Wait five minutes and they'll all be out of here. Like they got a train to catch."

She splashed soup in bowls, set them on a tray, and raced back to the table. I peeked out after her. Lieber hooted while Mayor Krank sketched on a napkin. The room was dark, lit by a single bulb and choked with cigarette smoke. Mary strode to the table, her wide hips swinging under her dress.

At noon coins jangled on the tabletop. The mayor pinned me against the counter with his belly and pumped my hand again on his way out. "Grateful for your support," he said.

"From him no such thing you got," Lieber claimed. Their argument swept them through the door. Mary fell on a chair, exhausted. We were alone.

"So you see what I been doing," she said. "How about you? Saved anybody today?"

"That doesn't sound like a serious question."

"It isn't."

"Well, that's my job."

She laughed, wiping her neck with a dishrag and pushing back her hair.

"It's a dying place," she said. "In case you didn't notice. It doesn't matter how many signs Krank puts up. Because of the cars. People used to come here in the train all summer. Row on the lake. Fish. Make a vacation of it. Now it's too close, too familiar. They can drive up north. Get bit by bigger mosquitoes. People here are more worried about saving their business than saving their souls. You'll see."

She leaned toward me, picking a fleck of lint from my cassock.

"I went to see Alois Pentz yesterday," I told her.

"So you're starting with the easy cases." There was a gap between her front teeth that showed when she smiled.

"What do you mean?" I said, defensive.

"What doesn't he believe? The way he tells it his mother comes back to look over the place. A ghost."

"He didn't say."

"That's what I hear."

"He asked about you."

She twisted the towel in her hand and threw it toward the sink. "'Now that's an old song. My boys need a man. Right?"

"Sort of." Her eyes tightened like her mother's, and her lips set in a hard line. We sat quietly for what seemed a long time.

"I had one and I don't know that I need another. We had eighty acres and a house where a human being could just barely live. I filled the holes in the plaster and I painted the walls and I scrubbed the floors until my fingers turned blue. I helped pull the calves out of the cows and I helped shovel out the barn. And I listened to him yammer. About whether this was what he was put on earth to do, to drain milk from a cow and grow hay to put in its mouth and smell cow shit every day of his life. I couldn't stand to hear it one more time—it makes me sick just to remember. Maybe it isn't why he was put on earth but that's what he was doing. So why couldn't he just do it? Why couldn't he just stop dreaming about what he could do and do what he was doing? There was enough to love in it. The green in spring and the rain and the corn gold in fall. He didn't see none of that.

"So he left. As I'm sure you already heard. And I got the boys and the farm, not that much of it was ours. The bank got most of it quick enough. Which is why I'm sitting here right now, wondering if I'll get supper ready in time. And why I'm living with my mother. And why I'm wondering what my boys are getting into when I'm not there to watch them.

"For the longest time I thought it was me. Now I tell myself that can't be true. It's because he wasn't grown and will never be grown. Because he didn't have any idea of how to live the days as they came. He thought there was always something better, that something else was waiting for him. It wasn't my fault. It wasn't me. It wasn't."

Her certainty was what made me doubt. I could hear her husband's version: She never let up. She never let me dream. She forced my nose into what we had and never let me get a breath of something better. She squeezed and squeezed, hoping to crush it out of me. And before she was able to do it I left. I left while there was still life left in me.

"Alois told me to ask," I said. "The way he took care of his mother, you've got to count that for something."

She laughed again, a sharp, bitter gasp. "God, would people laugh. A drunk for a father and a husband who walks away and then ending up with Alois."

"Decide what you want for yourself," I said weakly. "Run your own life."

"This ain't the city," she said. "I can't move to another part of town where they don't know me. Everybody knows everything and they don't forget nothing. You can go back where you came from. There's no place else for me."

She picked up a paring knife and started peeling potatoes, dropping them into the simmering pot. "Go save someone else," she said. "I'm not interested right now." When I stood to leave she didn't look up. The kitchen screen door squeaked, then slammed against the frame.

Mourning doves murmured on the wires. A gang of boys conspired on a corner. I imagined a wrinkled gossip behind every window curtain, watching, waiting. Hoping to see something, anything, and hoping to pull it apart.

LET ME IGNORE POOR SCHNEIDER FOR A MOMENT WHILE I speak my mind. To the boy I'm a relic, a fossil. My past is not quite imaginable, no matter how desperately I struggle to explain. He accepts the fact of my life—after all, I

breathe beside him—but he can't hear a single note of the
music.

I'm not saying I was any wiser. I stood on the edge of
disaster, not realizing the next step would carry me out into
thin air. I didn't even stop to consider it. Instead I busied
myself with prayer, which is to say I daydreamed.

Anything could set me off. That afternoon I sat in a hard,
wooden pew in my church, picking idly through a missal.
There in Genesis I bumped into Eve. Beautiful Eve, naked in
the wilderness, plucking fruit from the low branches. And
didn't she bear a striking resemblance to Mary Moon? That
sturdy frame, those broad feet; I unraveled her hair and let it
fall across her shoulders. I threw her stained apron behind a
rock, lifted the faded dress over her head. I pushed my
tongue between her gapped teeth. The curve of her breasts,
the sun on her back, her soles planted firmly on the dark soil
of Eden; she was perfect except that she lacked an Adam.
Will anyone volunteer? Here, right here! Make me a spindly-
legged Adam with smooth cheeks and pale flesh, an Adam
who can count his ribs and know when one is missing.

As I say, I prayed. Thy will, Lord, not mine. Though if
You care to take my will into consideration, then how about
an afternoon with my Eve? Just a few hours to caress her
belly, to explore her thighs, to bury myself in her breasts?
Give me an Eden, Lord, where the apple trees haven't
blossomed and serpents can't say a word. Then return me to
my own orchard, where the tiny green apples already hang
on the branches.

You could say a serpent crawled up my belly, and even if
it couldn't utter a word, still it throbbed with a familiar
message. Want and guilt, want and guilt, like the beat of a
heart or the flow of blood in the veins, one chained to the
other forever.

A door opened. A nun moved noiselessly to the sacristy.
She picked wilted white hydrangeas from the altar vases and
dropped them into a can. Each stem rapped against the metal
like a drumstick on a snare. I felt weak, as though my flesh
had grown too heavy for my muscles.

The nun turned toward me. It was Sister Perpetua, her pink, scrubbed face encased by the black habit. She walked down the aisle, cradling the dead white flowers in her arms.

"So you've been here, let's see, almost five days now, Father," she said, smiling vacantly.

"No, it's at least five years."

She laughed too loudly and covered her mouth. "That's what I thought at first. Now a year is what a week was. You'll see what I mean."

"I'm not sure I want to."

"Believe me, you'll be happier that way." She laughed again and walked away, a trail of brown petals scattering behind her.

I tugged at the skin bunched around my belt, trying to remember if there had been less of it. I resented being fattened like a pig for slaughter.

I took out my rosary to pray. My mind slipped away again before I hit the second decade. Alois's lake. The deep, cold water. Water black as the beads in my hand. Swimming deeper and deeper, away from it all. I have no idea how long I sat there.

"FINALLY," MRS. MOON COMPLAINED WHEN I RETURNED. "Supper is getting cold."

FRIDAY

I HAVE IN MIND AN ACT OF GOD. THEN AGAIN, WHAT ELSE IS there? I'm in the religion business, after all, not insurance. My company defines the term broadly. Act of God, in particular but not limited to: avalanche, blizzard, comet, earthquake, fire, flood, hail, hurricane, meteor, tsunami, and not excluding death (lingering and swift), illness (mental and physical), infertility, poverty, and excessive wealth. In which case the Company and its representatives may or may not be held liable, according to how we see fit.

An act of God, as I say, one that occurred years after the events I'm describing. Or attempting to describe, which is closer to the truth. How can I explain what happened? I barely knew where I was. I looked at a run-down village full of strangers and wondered what they thought and what they believed and why they did the things they did. And I didn't have a clue. I concocted theories that explained nothing and repeated these fairy tales to myself at night until I fell asleep.

Would you do any better? Forget about the hundreds of others and consider just Mrs. Moon. Bitter old hag, I thought at first. She's had her share of hard luck, no denying that. Still, what is her excuse? There's life in her and she's in her right mind, sour as it is. She could do worse than that.

Yes, her husband was shiftless, her child a disappointment, her grandchildren demons, and her work drudgery. A dismal biography, but hardly complete. Years later I saw a picture of her as a child. Her smile was skewed, plucky, and her little eyes full of mischief. And decades later—she lived to ninety-nine—Mrs. Moon was serene, almost saintly. She was alone in her rotting house, reading the newspapers with a magnifying glass while a radio blared on her kitchen counter. Long of tooth and ear and nose, her hair gone first completely white and then beyond that to yellow, she sat in her overheated parlor, at peace in her own world. Finally she had answered her true call. She was at heart a contemplative. Laugh, but it's true. Not quite a Teresa of Avila—her mean streak was too broad and deep for that—but certainly content with simplicity, celibacy, and silence. She was so deaf she barely heard the radio that yowled on her counter; her eyes were so cloudy that I doubt she saw anything on the page ahead of her. What could she do in the blurred quiet but breathe and pray?

Mrs. Moon was not born anew in her old age. Whatever she became, the seed of it existed within her when we first met. A mustard seed maybe, but still it was there. Her vileness—the word isn't too harsh—was born of the struggle between her nature and the conditions of her life. When this battle ended she was transformed into the person she was meant to be.

And me? During that week I was as blithering as Schneider. My stomach burbled constantly. I was usually lightheaded, my senses heightened by bad nerves. When I remember those days I believe the water was sweeter and the sky bluer and the human heart more frail. It was, as I say, a long time ago.

Oh, but I've done it again—set out on a walk around the block and ended up in China. The rivets have popped from my attention span. I get impatient, I get bored. A thousand-voice choir sings in my head. There's scarcely time to think one thought before another demands to be heard.

An act of God. An event beyond understanding. That which ridicules order and planning. Such as conception, say, or cancer, or the warmth of the sun on a late fall day. But in this case it's a tornado that's on my mind, a graceful funnel that bore down on St. Jude. The thin spout dropped from the green clouds and swept slowly across the land. Imagine a waltz playing in the background, the cloud's tail swaying in three-quarter time. And up close? Pandemonium. Dirt and tree limbs and washtubs and small animals and God-knows-what-all-else flew through the ugly sky, everything tossed aside as senselessly as it was carried off. I bring it up now only because it reminds me of Louise Thuen's wedding.

FRIDAY AFTERNOON THE BRIDE THREW OPEN THE FRONT doors of the church and charged inside. "It all goes right up by the altar," she said, a hysterical edge in her voice. Leon and her father struggled up the stairs after her, their faces hidden by bunches of wild lilies. The petals were orange, spotted with brown and streaked with yellow. Tiger lilies.

"I got bugs crawling in my nose," Leon grunted.

"I told you we shoulda bought flowers."

"For that money I could buy three cows." I couldn't see much of her but her father but his feet.

"Daddy," Louise whined. "We did it your way—these don't cost nothing." She seemed ready either to cry or to strangle someone. "You want to get the vases now or should we use milk cans?"

Through the church doors I saw the lake sparkling at the bottom of the hill. I made a run for it. Louise called my name as the door closed behind me.

The street ended at a dock where boats for rent were tied. They were of a type I haven't seen for decades, wooden rowboats resting lightly on the water, sterns and bows curved toward heaven. I peeled off my socks and dangled both feet in the water. The sun played on the lake's surface, warming my back.

Somewhere there is a scientist who thinks he can explain what happened to me. He tugs on his lab coat, scribbles on his blackboard, and proclaims that the pattern of light, the intensity—it stimulates the flow of hormones deep inside the brain, creating the feeling we typically label euphoric.

But oh! The pattern of light, its intensity, the golden sand shimmering below my feet, the breeze against my skin, the sun's heat, the cold, black water the blue waves hid, my heart's pumping, the warm blood in my veins, the music in my head, my being finally focused on a single point of light that shone most brightly, a point that explained with perfect eloquence the perfection of all existence, that is what I felt and understood, if only for an instant that I have tried for decades to recreate. I was overwhelmed by an art beyond art, painted on a thousand planes at once, the music made from the very breath in my lungs, the entirety of it gone without a trace, even though it continues to engulf me.

A gull landed on a post and squawked. I started, turned, and looked into its eyes. The black points gave away nothing. With another cry, the bird was off.

I tied my shoes and walked out of town. I walked without thinking, my mind wiped blank of Louise in the church and Ernst Moon in his grave and all the other ignorance, frailty, and heartache that is also part of creation.

I'm a believer but I'm not blind. There's plenty I'm determined not to see.

"THERE HE IS!" LOUISE SHRIEKED WHEN I RETURNED. SHE pointed a long finger my way. Leon planted a hand on my shoulder and steered me toward the altar.

"We got a picture problem, Father," he said. "You ain't in any of them. Louise says there ain't much time left." Leon stuck his thumb inside his collar and craned his neck. I threw on my vestments.

The photographer's head was smooth as a flashbulb. "Over here, Padre," he said, working a mouthful of snuff. He was from out of town.

Leon and Louise knelt before me at the foot of the altar. A white veil hid her face and trailed down her back. She scrutinized the altar, Leon, me. Each of you, her expression said, every last one, you're all too hopeless to criticize. Nothing to do but endure, ignore, pretend this is a world that deserves me.

"Okay, Padre," the photographer said. "Try to look, you know, religious." He wiped brown dribble from his lips. "Now hold up your right hand and look at the groom."

He who is about to be overwhelmed. Louise swept dandruff from his shoulder while he twisted inside his suit. Someday, I thought, he will sit down exhausted from another day in the fields. His children will crawl over his lap. Louise will yell from another room. And he'll wonder, what if I had run screaming from the church? Would the end of it have been better? Or only different? He'll look at the boy in the picture, the one with the jug-handle ears and the full head of hair, the person he once was, and ask what it was he thought he wanted. Then the cows will bellow again, aching to be milked. And Leon will pull on his boots, lurching through the straw and manure with a bucket in his hands, satisfying his herd for a few hours more.

The flash blinded us all. "Okay, Okay," the photographer said. "That oughta do it. Everything's beautiful. Best wishes."

Louise moaned. "We don't got ten minutes before people start coming." She turned to the bridesmaids flocked nearby, giggling among themselves. "Come on, girls," Louise said. "We gotta disappear. Grab the train." She bustled down the aisle pursued by her retinue. Leon shook his head and followed me into the sacristy.

"How are you feeling?" I asked him.

"I don't know," he said. "I don't know."

A few minutes later he stood at the altar, sweat dripping off his lip. For better, for worse, for richer, for poorer, in sickness and in health until death do you part? Louise gripped his hand, her knuckles squeezed white. He tugged at his ear.

"Thy wife shall be as a fruitful vine on the sides of thy house," I said, "and thy children as olive plants round about thy table."

Thy brethren shall gossip about you all the days of your life. "Ja, Louise," they'll say, "she got that man where she wants him." Thy days shall be marked by the screams of babes.

"If there be an objection," I said, "speak now or forever hold your peace." I listened to the silence. Wilbert Thuen studied his hands, no doubt fearing the total bill would appear there, like stigmata. Leon's mother gouged at her eyes with a handkerchief. His friends smirked, imagining the response they would never dare shout.

"May you see your children's children even to the third and fourth generation," I said. Mrs. Moon's crooked finger traced the words in her missal. Mary and Alois stood with her in the pew. Mary stared straight ahead, impossible to read. Alois looked as though he had just invented happiness. The altar boys mumbled something close to *"Deo gratias"* and the mass was over.

I can't say I was jealous—how could I admit it?—but for the next few hours I wondered what Alois and Mary were doing together. Was it some usher's idea of a joke?

TWO HARD FINGERS PINCHED DOWN ON MY ELBOW. "SAYING your prayers, Father?" The thick wine Mrs. Moon drank had stained her teeth purple.

"I'd be the only one," I said. My parish looked like an inbred tribe of cannibals, all dressed in mission clothes, all immune to Christianity. They filled the reception hall, thick-browed, big-nosed, ruddy, the smell of their sweat and smoke trapped against the low ceiling. They laughed and yodeled and shouted, their mouths full of sharp teeth. I had fled to a corner.

"You don't get smarter talking to yourself." Mrs. Moon picked a target from the mob. "Over there," she hissed in my ear. "What do you think that is?" She pointed at a farm boy whose wrists dangled from his sleeves.

"How should I know?"

Her fingers squeezed down harder. "Look at the ears! Like what? A donkey. Or a rabbit. They breed like rabbits. What family's got ears like that? Think! It's a Wegner for sure. Why you think Leon got married?"

"Because of his ears?"

"Because of his brothers! That boy wouldn't inherit more than the outhouse from his father. If he was going to get a farm he had to buy one or marry one. He got too many brothers ahead of him."

"That's what Louise said."

"Well, she ain't exactly the Virgin Mary if you know what I mean."

"I don't want to hear."

"Let's say she's a field been plowed before." She drained her tumbler. "And the seeds are coming up."

"What about Mary?" I said.

"What do you mean?" She turned those hard eyes on me, and her wicked grin evaporated.

"With Alois. I saw her with Alois." I pointed to them across the room, sitting together, speechless.

Mrs. Moon muttered something in German.

"I didn't think Mary was interested." She ignored me. "I didn't think she was interested," I repeated, nearly shouting.

"In what?" she snapped.

"Alois. What changed her mind?"

"How should I know?" Her face tightened and her eyes disappeared in furrows of dry skin. "This is the first time." She dragged me toward the buffet to end the discussion.

"But what do you think?"

"About what!"

"About if it will work out."

"Ach," she said, disgusted. "Look at him."

Alois loaded his fork, jammed it inside his mouth, and wiped his lips with the back of his hand. Mrs. Moon grimaced. "It gives me heartburn to watch."

Alois leaned toward Mary. He said something and looked to her, full of hope. She stared at him blankly. He turned back to his plate.

"I wonder what they're talking about?" I said to Mrs. Moon.

She took a deep breath.

"Who knows what goes on between people? At first Ernst

and me said anything that came to our heads. One thing was the same as the next. Anything to keep talking. The lights went off in the house, and there wasn't nothing to hear but the porch swing creaking and the bugs, every bug in the world, millions of them. We whispered to each other for hours."

Once she got going the words tumbled after each other, steadily increasing in velocity until they became impossible to stop.

"When I come in my mother said, 'What you been doing out there?'

" 'Talking,' I said.

"And she said, 'Talking about what?' My father is just snoring now.

" 'About nothing,' I said.

" 'Make sure nothing don't make you pregnant.'

" 'We didn't do nothing but talk.' I lied but it didn't make no difference because she knew it was a lie since she did the same herself."

Mrs. Moon handed me a plate and led me around the table. I took a piece of ham and she slapped another down beside it. She built a mountain of mashed potatoes on my plate and filled it with gravy. "I can feed myself," I said. She dropped a candied apple beside my potatoes. On her own plate a dozen peas rolled loosely around a sliver of ham.

We sat at a long table covered with white butcher paper. Mrs. Moon picked up her spoon and began hammering on her glass. I looked at my housekeeper and guessed she had gone insane. Her hair defied her comb, rising in a wild corona around her face. Her eyes gleamed and her face burned, first red, and then nearly purple. She bent over the water glass, beating it with tiny, relentless strokes. Her neighbors joined in, then their neighbors, then the whole hall, all hammering wildly, turning Mrs. Moon's ridiculous tattoo into a maddening swell.

"Go on," Mrs. Moon shouted. "Kiss her!" She grabbed another glass of wine.

Louise pulled Leon up by his lapels. She dug her fingers

into his hair and seemed to bite at his mouth, engulfing it
with her thick, red lips. The crowd hooted, happy savages.
Louise planted her hands on her hips, triumphant. Leon sat
down quickly and leaned over his plate.

Sheriff Kropp pushed his way to the head table and bellowed, "Quiet! A toast. A toast!" He was stuffed into a blue
uniform with a double row of brass buttons. His fringe of
hair stood on end; his face was inflamed.

"He's like this when the beer is free," Mrs. Moon whispered.

"I speak as the godfather of this lovely bride," Kropp said.
"A godfather who has hoped and prayed from the day she
was born. Praying I'd live to see this. Her wedding. The
beautiful bride. A handsome groom." He lifted a glass, soak-
ing his sleeve with beer. Kropp pulled a handkerchief from
his pocket and dabbed at his eyes.

"A toast!" he shouted. "That they're blessed! With as
many children as me! With as much as I have and more!"
Kropp drained his beer in a gulp.

"He ain't my godfather," Louise protested.

"Hush," her mother said. "There's no use arguing with
him when he's this way." Kropp dried his eyes again and
kissed the bride.

THE HALL WAS BUILT OF LOGS VARNISHED TO THE COLOR OF
honey. The ceiling was low, the light dim. Strangers appeared beside me, clapping my back and filling my glass.
The more they drank the less I was able to tell one from the
other. The beer made their faces into masks, flushed and
distorted, indistinguishable. So this is my flock I thought,
shuddering.

Lieber stepped out of the throng, a cigar stuck in his
mouth and beer trickling down his chin.

"Now you see here how much work for a priest there is?"
The words came out in a slur. "Stay sober and say for us
plenty of prayers!" He jammed a cigar in my pocket and
spilled beer on my shoes. Then he edged closer. "And Fa-

ther," he said, confidential. "For our friend Alois, too, you
should pray."

"What do you mean?"

"The Moon girl." He rolled his eyes.

"What?" I wasn't sure I wanted to know.

"I don't believe you they didn't tell," he said, flustered
now. "About her and our Father Unger? Before you came, in
the city they must have told you the reason."

"I don't know what you're talking about."

"Well, it's not to say then neither for me." Lieber swiped
nervously at his head, pushing back the nonexistent hair.
"But they didn't tell you?" He fidgeted for a moment, trying
to think. "More beer," he decided, lifting his glass. He was
gone.

I thought of frail old Unger and the package in his desk
and the pale round Eve who looked so much like Mary and
the soft touch of her hip against my ribs. And I was certain I
knew what Lieber wanted to say.

Where was she now? I needed to look at her with the scales
gone from my eyes.

LOUISE CLIMBED THE BANDSTAND IN THE SMOKE AND HEAT,
waiting for the crowd to close in around her. She hiked up
her dress and slid a blue garter off her leg, the same leg that
was cut off thirty years later after our town doctor botched a
routine wart removal. A minor infection led to a dark, streaked,
gangrenous mess, which led to an amputation. But the leg on
stage remains the everlasting limb of memory, the ankle
impossibly narrow, the calf finely tapered, and the thigh, the
thigh, oh, what a lush paradise it suggested. She tossed the
lace garter into the crowd, setting off a tangle of hands and
arms, everyone grabbing for the scrap at once. Louise threw
back her head and laughed, her wide glistening lips pulled
back so far I saw her gums.

The band began to play. A trumpeter blew hard to cut
through the din, veins bulging at his temples. As a tuba and
accordion joined in the tables were pushed toward the walls.

I watched the first dance from my dark corner. Louise led Leon, her veil wrapping around them as they turned. The druggist Krank swept up Mrs. Moon. Her arthritic goose-step was cured, the tight corners of her mouth loosened. For an instant I saw her daughter, too, her hand slipped low on Alois's back as he led in an oafish step. I resented them both—Alois for the possibilities before him, Mary for the tilt of her neck, for the red hair that fell from her head, for the swell of her breasts and hips. For the temptation she presented and for all old Unger suffered and enjoyed. I peered out from my corner, twisting my head to follow them.

"Looking for me?" Louise stood at my side, breathless. "Dance?" she said. Before I had a chance to refuse, she set my hand on the curve of her waist. The trumpeter attacked the music again.

Louise didn't follow, or was it that I didn't lead? She turned me in a pair of tight circles, then took us in a wide loop around the floor. The ceiling tilted and the lights made a dizzy orbit and my neck throbbed against my priest's collar. Sweat dropped from Louise's forehead and ran down her bare neck into the bodice of her gown. We twirled once, twice, then once again. I could have sworn she bit my ear.

"Too bad I met Leon first," she said, her voice dusky and soaked with brandy. "I could have gone for somebody, you know, spiritual." Leon hurried toward us.

She kissed him, winking at me. Mrs. Moon cackled like the devil and pinched my arm again. "You need to make a confession," she screeched, happy at last.

LET ME STOP HERE TO CATCH MY BREATH WHILE THE MUSIC still plays, while the drunken crowd roars, while Alois and Mary eye each other furtively, and imagine the life they might live together. Do you wonder how they might have lived? Because it must be clear to everyone, even to poor, dull Schneider, who at this moment fusses with his watch, that Alois and Mary did not—could not—live as man and wife. Where would the story be in that? Man and woman meet and live more or less happily ever after. An everyday tale, common as dirt. Why would I waste my breath?

But a story of love gone wrong, or, better yet, of the impossibility of love, now that's another matter. Two people breathe the same air and eat the same food and they want, each of them, not to live alone and not to die alone and not to fade from the memory of the world. Yet they can't save each other from that which they most fear. Why, short of a routine miracle, isn't this the familiar story?

But wait now, Schneider stirs! He opens his mouth, hesitates, closes it again, thinks—I'm guessing, understand—and asks, "Why did she go with him?"

"Who?"

"The girl. Mary." When even the smallest thought echoes in the boy's brain I want to embrace him.

Years after that night had ended I asked Mary Moon the same question. Her hair was gray by then, and she had spread out in all directions. She answered immediately, not stopping for a moment to consider. "Spite," she said, so certainly that I did not think to ask what score she was settling.

"WILL YOU BE NEEDING A RIDE HOME, FATHER?" LEON ASKED. "I mean, later?" He did an imitation of sobriety, nodding at what I said and repeating it. "Leaving now? Walking?" His head bobbed slowly. I shook his hand and stooped to kiss Louise. Drunk, she grinned lasciviously.

In the night the band music faded and the insects took over. The moon skimmed the treetops. I hummed a polka to myself, empty-headed and happy until I spotted a couple on the road ahead of me. Alois and Mary. Her arms were crossed beneath her breasts, her head cast down. Alois squeezed his hands into fists then loosened them again.

"Ain't it a beautiful night," he said.

"Beautiful," I answered.

"Looks like it might rain yet tonight," Mary said. The harsh edge of her voice was muted. We all stared at a broad wall of clouds that rose in the west, gray against the black sky.

"That'd be good for the crops, I guess," I said.

Alois rubbed the back of his neck. "We sure could use it," he replied. We stood peering at each other in the darkness, silent and stupid as the trees.

"We oughta be getting back," Mary said. Her hair swept over the side of her face. She brushed it back with one hand and crossed her arms again. In the moonlight her face was like marble.

I wanted to scream. We had no more power to communicate than the bugs that chirped in the ditch. Why did we bother to talk? How much less could we know about each other? How much more could we keep from ourselves?

Could you live together? That's what I wanted to shout. Could you stand each other for days and weeks and years? Could you bring children into the world and raise them? Could you comfort each other in old age? And if you can't, then what will you do? Will there be anyone else for either of you? Will you grow more eccentric, more difficult to satisfy, until you are finally, irredeemably, alone?

Alois lifted an arm as though he intended to drape it across Mary's shoulder. He let it fall again to his side. They walked down the road together, careful not to brush against each other. I watched until they were lost in the shadows along the road, stifling the last question that I wanted so badly to shout.

What about Father Unger? How much of her did he have, and how much did he regret?

As I walked to town the moon rose, its light cutting through the darkness. The apple trees cast shadows on the grass outside my window. Unripened fruit shone in the silver light.

I pulled a chair to the window and looked out over the orchard. The night was gray and black. Branches jerked, the leaves shook. I thought I saw something move among the trees. A shadow, a bird, an animal. Nothing at all.

I was an exile, left alone to imagine the course of the night. Maybe Louise had already nodded at Leon, signaling him that it was time to act out the plot they planned days before. They slip out the door separately and meet at the car. He reaches underneath it to cut loose the cans that are certainly tied there. Then they drive, slowly at first, without the lights, sneaking toward the road, stealing away toward the room he has rented fifteen miles down the highway. For the first time they will have a bed of their own, a bed that sags on metal springs and is too small. The bedspread is a dingy green, the wallpaper stained. But Leon pays no mind. He kicks off his shoes and tears at his coat. He walks to his wife, who stands before the hazy mirror. His arms reach around her to smooth the belly that is already beginning to swell. One hand rises to caress a breast ripening with pregnancy. She reaches behind herself, pulling his leg against hers, those soft, thick lips twisting with a sad smile that she does not quite understand and that he ignores.

And Mrs. Moon, the last song fading now, feels the stiffness set into her limbs again as the grace she briefly possessed tightens into a hard knot in her stomach. She instinctively gathers up a load of dishes and drops them again in disgust, remembering that this time others are paid for the task.

Lieber pats his breast pocket, searching for another cigar, realizing he gave the last away hours ago. He wishes that the music still played, that the beer still flowed from the kegs, that his head did not throb, that the night would last forever and that tomorrow, with its endless inventory of potatoes and tomatoes and gray, rotting meat, would never come.

And maybe, if our God is a merciful God and the angels intervene, Alois finds the right words to say to Mary. He takes her back to her porch where they sit, his big arm stretched around her shoulders. Mrs. Moon, awake in her bed, quakes with the desire to get her daughter inside. Reluctantly remembering her own youth, she decides finally, miraculously, to hold her tongue.

BUT THE LIFE OF ST. JUDE, I TELL SCHNEIDER, SURPASSED MY ability to imagine it. He chews his gum, listening as little as possible. It may be Christian to indulge an old man, he thinks, but listen to this one rattle on! He checks his watch and wonders when he will be delivered.

Schneider of the digital watch! Most innocent Schneider of the unreasoning microchip! How incapable he is of seeing that the changes in this world are superficial. Schneider tells me that his watch can measure his pulse, but what good will it do him when that watch is strapped to a pulseless wrist? Will its alarm go off and bring back his soul from wherever it has fled? Loneliness and longing, guilt, fear, and death: can Schneider show me the little buttons he presses to control them? What, really, has changed?

That night I sat in my room, too excited to sleep. I sat at the window for what seemed like hours, the lace curtain brushing against my cheek.

What if it was true, what Lieber said? Then, in my very bed, perhaps, Mary and Unger . . . But no, not with her mother banging in the kitchen. They must have gone somewhere else. Into the church itself? The basement, that's where I'd take her. Of course, I'm not taking her anywhere. But could that be what she meant, the way she looked at me in the restaurant? The way her hip brushed against my ribs? With Unger's package still in the desk anything is possible. Unimaginable coitus. The marriage act. Lord knows I wouldn't be the first.

After hours of this my head sunk into the chair's cushion. I believe I slept. I dreamed that quiet laughter rose from the apple branches. My parishioners danced from tree to tree, murmuring as they stripped off their clothes. They rolled naked in the black grass, ran up to my window to peer in and point, disappearing only when Mrs. Moon's voice sounded in the darkness. I awoke.

Mary trailed her mother through the trees. They stood on the steps whispering until Mrs. Moon hammered on the door. I opened it just as she raised her fist again.

Her hair was wild and her dress was wrinkled, as though she had slept in it. I saw a predatory gleam in her eyes. The shoulder of Mary's dress was torn and a thin scratch ran down one cheek.

"We gotta figure out what to do," Mrs. Moon said, her voice a rasp.

"What's the . . ."

"Mary's been attacked."

"That's not exactly what happened, Momma."

"Then your dress ripped itself?"

"It's just that he . . ."

"I say Kropp should arrest him." Mrs. Moon slapped her hand against the door frame.

"Mary," I said. "What happened?"

"I don't know what to . . ."

"Go on. Tell him." She glared at her daughter.

"Mrs. Moon," I said softly. She dug her nails into her own arm.

Mary tried to pull the torn cotton fabric together but it slid down her arm again. A few threads strayed across her skin, white on white. She pushed back her hair and then spoke in a halting voice all but drowned by the wind in the leaves.

"We walked back to the hall. We walked a while and he put his arm around me. I didn't tell him no. He didn't say a word. We just walked." She fidgeted with her purse.

"They played a waltz, slow, and we danced. 'It's been so long since somebody held me.' That's what he said. Everybody had been drinking all night and it was late. They were ready to go home after they danced this last slow one. The wind came off the lake and blew through the hall. It was, I don't know. Romantic. Even with him it was romantic.

"When the music stopped we sat by the door. We each had a glass of beer and we sat there and we talked. About the kids. About his farm. That there's room. That we don't have to be alone. He told me about his mother, shaking so bad in the end that she couldn't hold a spoon. And so he fed her. She was helpless and he took care of her. He loved her. He could love somebody."

"And you believed him."

"Please, Mrs. Moon." I put my hand on her arm. She brushed it away.

"I'm tired of believing nothing."

The crickets sang, oblivious.

"But how . . ." I nodded at the torn dress.

"We walked down to the lake and sat by the rocks. He put his hand on my knee. We talked. He put his arm around me.

"He leaned against me and he kissed me and I opened my eyes and saw him and I realized again that he was pathetic, that if I thought anything else it was just the breeze and the waves and beer in my head. After years with those boys by myself and years of hauling food to a bunch of walruses and years of guessing at what everybody was saying about me, I wanted to believe something. But I couldn't believe that. I opened my eyes and I couldn't believe it. I couldn't forget who he was. I tried to tell myself this is a warm human body and that's enough but it wasn't.

"He started saying something, mumbling. About being together, really being together. Soft at first. I couldn't understand what he said. He put his head against my shoulder and balled my sleeve up in his fist. And it tore and I screamed. You can't do that with me, that's what I yelled, and he sat on his rock, looking at me like I stabbed him. 'Then what am I going to do,' he said. Pitiful. And when he was like that I thought he was one more man trying to get something over on me and I couldn't stand it. I told him I wasn't going to be raped by a farmer on a dark beach with beer on his breath, that I wasn't that young and stupid.

"He reached for me again and I pushed him away and saw his face and I was scared. He reached for my shoulder again and I hit him and he looked like a pig just stuck. He ran off with his big hands over his ears. I hollered after him again but he didn't stop running."

Mrs. Moon grabbed Mary's chin and jerked her head so their eyes met. "That's what happened?"

Mary looked at her mother, then at me, then at the trees

that stood in the dark grass. She turned her head. Her mother's hand dropped away.

No one spoke. I saw Alois running down the road, alone under the moon, those dull sleeping eyes finally opened by humiliation and fear and the empty future. He was alone. He would always be alone. Not even Adam was so cursed. He would live alone and die alone and his grave would go untended. His father's farm would crumple into the dirt. What thousands—millions!—of others accomplish so simply, he could not. The pygmies and the Eskimoes and the naked indians of the Amazon; they could find wives, but not him! There would never be a warm body beside his. He would never speak into the winter night and hear another voice confirm his existence. So he runs until sweat and dew glaze his face. His dog feels the noise a half mile off and howls as though hell had opened beneath him. The donkey wakes and wails. When Alois hears the noise his tears boil over, so bitter they seem to burn his face. I didn't mean nothing, he tells himself, a lie. I was lonely, that's all. The arm he stretched across her back was like part of her body, shifting with each breath she took. He wanted to suck in all her warmth and feel her hair against his face and forget about everything else. But he had no idea how to get the thing he wanted. He turns it over and over in his mind and he gets no further. His legs flail at the gravel road and the long weeds whip his legs. He is back again with his animals and his farm and the solitude that could eat him whole. Who would notice if he ran forever?

Mrs. Moon twisted her hands and ground her feet into the concrete step. Mary was planted there, impenetrable. "What do you want me to do?" I asked.

Mrs. Moon's chest rose. She exhaled sharply. "You tell me what you *can* do," she said. Then she snapped, "He shouldn't be walking around if he's attacking women."

"I can go talk to him tomorrow. We should hear his side."

"If you can't get him to explain, I'll get Kropp to handle it. He can think things over in jail."

The edge crept back into Mary's voice. "The whole town will know as soon as you tell Kropp."

Mrs. Moon sighed, venting a fraction of her rage. "Go talk to the fool," she told me. She turned to Mary. "We're going home."

I watched them walk away, Mrs. Moon clutching her daughter's arm. The two trails they left in the dew disappeared among the trees. I sank back into my chair. The moon set and the sun rose. I fell asleep to the symphony of bird song that played in the orchard.

SCHNEIDER'S JAW TWITCHES. A QUESTION BEGINS THE SLOW journey from his brain to his tongue. Poor Schneider; if he didn't remind me so much of myself, I wouldn't so often despise him.

It doesn't seem like such a big deal to me," he says. "Nothing really happened."

How do I explain to Schneider the Anonymous, Schneider of the Disposable Wristwatch? He who measures time by the hundredth of the second but is not haunted by his actions?

To the thousands of people who pass him in the street he is another face, as easily forgotten as all the others. He can murder his mother and poison her dog and even so, soon enough, he will be replaced in the popular imagination. Some other moron will improve on the outrage by eating his murdered mother's dead dog, reaping a small headline on an inside page for his efforts.

In St. Jude his actions would never be forgotten. There the raw clay of any event, no matter how dimly perceived or understood, was shaped with each new telling, built into the thing it should have been. The years smoothed out the harsh edge of fact until the story became perfect. Everything was distorted but nothing was forgotten. The imaginary history followed its characters to their grave and beyond.

As the sun rose the court of gossip held its first session. How did that Moon girl get scratched up? Why did she and the old lady talk to the priest so late last night? Wasn't she with Alois at the wedding? Didn't you always take him for harmless? It don't seem like nothing you'd accuse him of, rape, not that you can ever really tell the type. But you tell me what she was doing with him in the first place. I suppose you could see it coming. You remember her father, Ernst Moon. And her husband, that one that just walked off. And, well, I suppose you heard about her and the old priest.

"Let me put it this way," I tell Schneider. "What if your parish believed you buggered altar boys? You couldn't convince them otherwise and you couldn't leave. What would you do?"

Schneider wonders, I suppose, if vulgarity is a symptom of Alzheimer's disease. Old-timer's disease, as I thought the nurse said the first time I heard the phrase. She dared to apply it to me, whispering her diagnosis to a young twit of a doctor a third my age. Let them see how much patience *they* have for a nursing home full of empty prattling when they reach my age.

Which is not to say I'm unaware of my many blessings. I thank God daily for Schneider's sanctimoniousness. It makes him such an easy instrument to play.

"Altar boys?" Schneider says. "Geez."

SATURDAY

MRS. MOON'S FIRST NAME WAS ALMA, A POINT I MAKE ONLY to show how my mind works these days. Meaningless details bubble up through my gray matter. I can't remember my doctor's name, but I can tell you that my razor back then was a brass Gillette. And the pen I used to write my pastor's report at the end of that first week? A burgundy Schaeffer that smudged my fingers. Inky blots, like sin.

I never called her Alma; that never crossed my mind. The ancient Jews would be quicker to pronounce the name of God. She was swollen, tidal. Her bosom strained against her cotton housedresses, her fat arms jiggled when she walked. She had no noticeable chin line, just wattles and a soft pouch of flesh that drooped toward her neck. And still, because of those cutting eyes and the hook in her nose, she seemed angular, sharp.

That morning at Mass she knelt among women so old their tongues had gone gray, women who tasted their mouths turning to dust. Trust me: I speak from personal experience. At the moment my palate feels like the Sinai.

"Who shall ascend unto the mountain of the Lord?" I asked them. "Who shall stand in His holy place?"

"The innocent of hands and clean of heart." A small crowd, in other words. Not much of anyone I know.

The first time I saw Alois I thought he might qualify. He

stood with his shovel in those giant hands—remember?
—throwing dirt into Ernst Moon's grave. The dying sun
shone into his eyes and his face was golden, wondering,
defiant of age and experience.

What changed my mind? His menacing strength? The
sound of his boot against his dog's ribs? That, yes, but also
his feigned helplessness, his indifference to decay, his disbe-
lief that anything must be earned. To a great extent his soul's
contour was defined by sloth.

But I also saw in him a blasphemous ache to claim part of
creation for his own, to use Mary Moon to prove to himself
that he existed. His greed for love was frightening. The
town's children sensed his desperation, recognizing it as no
different from their own. He poisoned his mother, they said,
sensing his passion but confusing its intent. Or perhaps understanding perfectly, feeling drawn toward murder themselves because they could never receive enough love to fill
their need. That which did not serve them utterly they
yearned to destroy.

In my church I sat hosts on those parched tongues, the
gray faces silently demanding I make good on a promise
we all wanted desperately to believe. Mrs. Moon was the last
of my communicants. Enraged, she devoured her host,
chewing at it as though to extract satisfaction.

KROPP WAITED FOR ME IN THE SACRISTY. THE FLAME IN HIS
complexion the night before had become a fishy pallor. White
stubble sprouted from his chin.

"Morning," he said, a complaint. I said the same to him.

Kropp looked baffled. "I hope not," he muttered.

"Good morning," I shouted.

"Oh, ja," Kropp said wearily. "Morning." He cocked his
good ear forward and peered at me with one bloodshot blue
eye. "What's the trouble with Alois?" he demanded, his voice
slowly reaching its usual pitch. "I heard. About the trouble."
He scratched at his fringe of hair.

"It wasn't six hours ago."

He shrugged.

"How did you find out?"

"Mary," Kropp said. "Saw her at the hotel. Scratch on her cheek. Asked her what happened. 'Nothing,' she said. Didn't say nothing more about it. Spotted Mrs. Moon on her way here this morning and asked her. She said, 'The priest is talking to that fool Alois today—that's all I got to say.' Then she marched off.

"I should go with you," Kropp said. "To see Alois." He nodded toward the window. His mud-splattered patrol car waited beneath the trees.

"We can't go to Alois's place in a police car. He's not Al Capone."

"Right!" Kropp exclaimed. "There's no telling."

"He's not Al Capone!" What had he heard?

"Ja, I suppose," Kropp said, disappointed. "So then what?"

"I'll go talk to him. Alone. There are things he might tell me that he'd never . . ."

Kropp cut me short. He rubbed his head and pulled at his nose and said, "Ja ja ja ja." He walked unsteadily toward the door. "Let me know," he said. "When you get back."

I TOOK UNGER'S BIKE FROM THE SHED AGAIN AND PEDALED through town. Lieber, sweeping his sidewalk, raised one hand in a somber salute. Smit stood in the window of his mortuary, watching me pass. Maybe they were dazed from the night before, capable of no more than clutching a broom or staring out a window. But I suspected—I feared—they were like dogs that had caught a distant scent. The air was infected. They were excited, distressed, fearful of what they might learn and eager to find out.

Do you think I exaggerate when I say the earth itself seemed feverish that day? The night's dew baked out of the grass and rose in clouds of hypnotizing heat. At the edge of town I decided I was sick—a headache, maybe the start of the flu. I should turn back, I thought, saying the words out loud to convince myself. Why ruin my health on a hopeless case?

Whatever I said to Alois the end would be the same. He would be left alone on his broken-down farm. The buzz of gossip would follow him forever: Did you hear what he did to the Moon girl? You could have figured him for the type, now isn't that right?

I passed the lineup of blackbirds in the swamp grass. Horseflies swirled around my bare head. Lieber's right, I thought. The heat will drive me crazy. The sun is cooking my brain, pushing the gray folds against my skull, crushing out thought. I was stewed. The bike clanked, the tires scratched against the gravel. Heat climbed in waves toward the gray misty clouds.

I heard Alois's ranting donkey long before I arrived. When I turned onto the mud track the animal raced for the fence, its purple tongue quivering toward heaven. The windmill blades stood still. The farm breathed exhaustion.

I banged on the screen door. A cat scrambled out an open window. I shouted Alois's name and pounded again. He didn't answer.

Fine, I thought. Fine. Time to think this through.

I rested against a rotting elm, listening for the slap of his worn boots. What would I say when he appeared? Trust in the Lord, the Lord who provides? What exactly had He provided lately in this farmyard full of ghosts?

I could feel them in the heavy air, the souls who built the barn, who massaged the cow's teats, who dragged stumps from the fields, who strung fences and picked rocks. Did they regret their labor, seeing the end to which it had come? Or was their work an end in itself, no more a choice than breathing?

I fell asleep, my head against a polished root that snaked out of the grass.

How much time passed? How much time does a dream require? More than an hour? Less than a second? Who was it that answered my questions?

Why did you do it?

I didn't do nothing.

But the girl is scratched and her dress is torn.

It wasn't me.

She says it was.

It was, all right, but that ain't me. How can I explain? She didn't have to come with me. She stayed. You know what they say about her.

That's not what we're talking about.

It is. You can't separate one from the other. You can't do it.

But . . .

Leave me alone. Just leave me alone. I got to answer to all of them that are here. That's enough. That's more than enough. I don't need you, too.

I WOKE AS ALOIS'S ROOSTER SCRATCHED AT THE DIRT BESIDE my hand. The bird focused on me with one eye, then twisted his head to see with the other. He pecked once lightly at my finger, then slammed his beak against the bone. I screamed as I scrambled to my feet.

I heard pigs grunting, cows bellowing in the barn.

"Alois," I cried. I hurried across the carpet of alfalfa that sloped down toward his lake. His dog lay in the grass under the tree, growling quietly as he watched me approach. I walked slowly to the lake's edge. The boat was gone.

I saw it floating far from shore, a small blot of red on the still water. I called his name again and listened to the echo from the opposite bank.

Say he floated on his back, his ears clogged with water, absorbed in the sound of his own breath. He might never hear me. Or, shamed and fearful, he might pretend not to hear, imagining that what he ignored would disappear. I sunk to the comfortless grass. The sun throbbed.

I tugged at my shoes, slipped out of my cassock. I stood naked on the shore, embraced by the moist heat.

Mr foot sunk into the mud at the lake's edge. With each step the muck grew colder, blacker. Gas rose from it, bubbling around my legs. I dove.

The pounding in my head stopped. My lungs cleared. I swam deep into the lake, where the water was colder still.

There was no sound, no shape, only the green algae drifting before my eyes. I sunk deeper, my foot settling into the silt at the lake's bottom. Black silt, rotting slowly in the silver-green twilight, cold as winter, insubstantial as snow, frightening beyond reason.

I thrashed to the surface again, lungs bursting with fear.

The willow branches hung still. The clouds floated dead in the air, a flat slate of gray. I turned on my back and drifted quietly.

When I settled in the grass to wipe the mud from my feet I found a black leech between my toes, its head fixed in the pale, wrinkled skin.

YEARS AFTER THESE EVENTS, AFTER THE TRUTH HAD LONG since been replaced by a glorious translation, I was visited by a fortune-teller who traveled with a ragtag carnival. Gypsies, we called them. They camped on the lakeshore each summer, holding shows that were lit by torchlight. During those warm nights the world was changed into a place where men swallowed fire, where women grew beards, where the future could be revealed. A better world for the most part, except that the gypsy children crawled in the dust, starving.

My fortune-teller was a strapping redhead in bib overalls, steeped in garlic and covered with freckles. She came to me for confession, insisting that it did her good. Exactly how or why was never clear to me, since her behavior grew less God-fearing with each passing year. She spelled out her sins in a soft whisper, lifting her brown eyes to measure my reaction.

"Fornication," she'd say, "another of my failings." A half-formed smile crossed her lips as she sighed. "I might as well admit to sodomy, too, and make a clean sweep." She raced into a loving description of her sins with the carnival contortionist, with the magician, with the contortionist and magician together, then asked me—mockery, this was—if I ever thought of running away.

She believed that some souls stick to this planet long after their bodies are dead. Their longing to leave this earth, their weariness, she said, it rubs off on the building in which the soul is trapped. The building itself becomes charged with such tension and sadness that it requires a rest. "You know what I'm talking about," she said, squeezing my thigh with a burning hand.

Yes, of course, I knew. The dry alfalfa crackled with every step I took toward Alois's farmyard. The house was bent with a greater load than its beams could carry. The door tilted, the steps sloped. The glass was so old that everything seen through the windows was distorted. I knocked on the door.

"Alois!"

No answer. I let myself in.

Drawn curtains dimmed the parlor. Lace doilies, yellow and torn, covered the heavy furniture. Clots of dust drifted on the floor.

In the dining room a china closet held a woman's sparse treasures: painted cups and saucers, a chipped vase, some wineglasses. The door leading out of the room was stuck, pinched shut by the wall that pushed down against the jamb. When I put my shoulder against it, the door flew open.

I stood in a bedroom that must have belonged to Alois's parents. The shades were drawn, the air still. The few furnishings were still carefully arranged, covered with dust.

A crucifix rested on a quilted bedspread.

A worn pair of men's black shoes were tucked under a dresser.

Brushes and cheap lotions stood in rows on a dressing table.

A rag rug, washed and mended, was laid beside the bed.

The painstaking organization spoke of a threadbare life in which every purchase was preceded by months of longing, scrimping, reconsideration. Then, finally, unbelievably, when the cheap relic was in hand, it became as much a burden as a pleasure, one more possession to be polished, maintained, and repaired, its useful life extended beyond reason.

A wedding picture hung above the bed. The photographer seemed to have roused the bride from a sleep that she left unwillingly. Her eyes were unfocused and a smile played at the corners of her full lips. She could only have been Alois's mother. But what peace could she have found with this groom? He was lean, his eyes were sharp, the brows a thin slash; here was a man full of plans that demanded endless labor. What house could hold them both? What kind of life would it be, pinched between these two? Their child could be one or the other but not a part of both, for there seemed no ground for compromise between them. Alois was his mother's child, leaving his father's farm to rot around him. But certainly he could not be deaf to his father's outrage as the buildings crumbled.

I found Alois's room on the second floor, up a narrow flight of stairs. A sheet was tangled at the foot of the bed. Soiled curtains hung slack beside an open window. The smell of the barn drifted from overalls heaped in a corner.

The nightstand held a Bible open to Genesis. Adam begat Seth, Seth begat Enosh, Enosh begat Kenan. On and on the web stretched, one strand ending with Alois alone on his yellowed sheets. Tell me, when the roots of a tree can sink no further, does the forest suffer? How sharp is the world's pain when a family dies? Do the souls of a thousand ancestors hector the last son, arguing against the obliteration of their memory?

I shouted Alois's name once more, expecting nothing. The word died in the dust and the quiet. I closed the door behind me and went back into the light.

A cow hanging heavy with milk spotted me in the yard and cried. The donkey sent up another protest, the sound of chaos. I fled as though from a revolt, the bike rattling down the pitted track.

From the hilltop Alois's farm was quiet again. The lake,

the weathered barn and grazing cows, the black shadows under the trees: it could have been a painting.

I hurried back toward town.

KROPP'S DESKTOP HELD A BADLY TANGLED FISHING REEL AND a knife. A single bulb dropped from the high ceiling, placed for some unfathomable reason directly over the doorway, where it lit Kropp's work feebly, if at all. A map of the county hung on the green wall behind the sheriff's desk.

Kropp himself was leaned back in a stout oak chair, his eyes closed. He ran a hand lightly over his few remaining hairs.

"Mr. Kropp," I said.

He purred.

"Mr. Kropp," I shouted. The bare room rang with the noise.

His eyelids drifted open. His hand fell to the back of his neck.

"I couldn't find him."

Kropp sat upright, struggling to snap me into focus. "Huh?" he said.

"Alois."

"Speak up!" He dug at his ear with his thumb.

"I couldn't find him!"

"Right," Kropp said, suddenly officious. "Couldn't find him. Probably ran away."

"I don't know." I moved closer and blared at what I assumed was his good ear.

"Where else could he be?" Kropp declared, pleased with this reasoning.

"His boat was on the lake. He wasn't in it."

"Drowned. He could have drowned."

"He's a fish in the water."

"Maybe it's to throw us off. So we think he drowned. Ran away for sure."

"From what? We don't know that he did anything."

"But he doesn't know that," Kropp said. He whisked the

fishing reel into a drawer and stood up. His chair banged against the wall.

"We should go investigate," Kropp said. "First thing tomorrow."

"Tomorrow?"

"Can't go before then. Baseball game after supper. I umpire. Never get back in time if we go now." Kropp dropped back into his squeaking chair.

"We leave after mass tomorrow," he said, and waved me out the door.

AT SUPPERTIME THE TOWN WAS QUIET. I RODE MY BIKE ON the south side of the street, clinging to the shadows. Lieber stood on the sidewalk, rolling up the awnings that shaded his shop windows. When he saw me coming he stopped and walked into the street.

"So," he said, waiting. "Ja."

"Hot day," I said.

"Ja, hot," he agreed, distracted. "So."

"Think it'll rain?"

Lieber ignored my question. He rested his hands on the handlebar. "So," he said slowly, "what happens with Alois? Me you can tell."

Vampires, I thought. All of them. What right did they have to know? Lieber rocked the bike gently back and forth, waiting for a reply.

"What I hear, let me tell you that," Lieber said, drawing closer to me. His cheeks glowed from the heat. Sweat dappled his white shirt. "Mary Moon, he, they say, well . . ." Lieber searched for a suitable term. "He *attacked* her," he said, whispering the word, implying that, though we both knew rape was the correct description, we agreed not to utter it upon the civilized streets of St. Jude.

"That is what people say. And her mother tells her not to tell, not to let anyone know. That's it? I promise again. Me you can tell."

"I don't know what happened," I said. "Alois didn't rape her." The word fell between us, an embarrassment.

Lieber stared quietly at the street for a moment. "Why then does all this news spread?" He was like a boy with a rock in his hand, standing before a sheet of glass. What joy, hearing it shatter.

"Idle minds," I said and shrugged. Lieber loosened his grip on my bike.

"But to Alois's farm, isn't that where you went? Didn't he explain? A priest he would tell."

"I couldn't find Alois. He must have been out in his fields."

"Ha," Lieber retorted. "To check how the weeds grow— how long does that take? So now he disappears, that's how it sounds to me."

Lieber wiped his hands on his apron and headed back into his store. "Tomorrow for the baptism, I see you then," he said, locking the door behind himself.

I HATE MY DOCTOR. HE POKES AND JABS AT ME, BANGING ON my ribs as though I were a melon left too long in the fields. "Looking fine, looking fine," he lies. "You'll outlive us all." He talks to me as if I'm a child. "Now let's see you walk," he says, merrily, merrily, everything a bright and happy game. I dodder down the hallway, spine twisted, legs dragging, my walker scraping against the linoleum. "Good, good, good," he proclaims. His name—I'm not making this up—is Slaughter. Dr. Alphonse Slaughter, specialist in geriatric orthopedics, holder of a wall full of degrees, a smooth-faced babe whose largest concern, no doubt, is his receding hairline. May he live to be one hundred and twenty. May his bones turn to mush.

In the hours before my appointments with him I watch the clock, willing time to stop. I notice every twitch, every spasm in my tired limbs. I feel pains I've never felt before. I fear this, finally, will be the visit where Slaughter shakes his head and says, "There's nothing we can do," before running off to his golf game.

Even so, I dreaded my appointment with Mrs. Moon even more than I now despise my ordeals with Slaughter. In the short distance between Lieber's store and Mrs. Moon's house all of nature argued against my progress, begging me to stop and notice. Birds sang songs I had never heard. Leaves trembled in the trees, creating magnificent walls of light and shadow. The pattern of dust in the street, the tire tracks and hoofprints: there alone was a life's worth of study. Why go on? Why not stop and let the rest of the world take care of itself?

MUCH AS A TREE'S AGE CAN BE TOLD FROM ITS RINGS, MRS. Moon's changing fortunes were revealed by the additions to her home. The lean-to kitchen that sprouted from the back was added when she and Ernst and Mary first moved in. "I'm gonna have a kitchen with running water," she proclaimed, and so Ernst set to building a lean-to that leaned more than it should have. The bedroom tacked on to the south side came after Mary moved back home with the boys. The porch stuck on the front, added just the year before, was Mrs. Moon's acknowledgment of her increasing age. She imagined herself retired, watching the traffic go by from her porch swing.

Mary's boys stood on a small patch of grass ahead of the porch, throwing a knife at a young tree. "Is your grandmother home?" I asked. Mike wiped the knife blade against his pants leg.

"I guess she's inside," he said lazily. Mrs. Moon appeared at the door.

"It's about time," she said.

She led me through her parlor, a dark room with a shabby rug and a few pieces of cast-off furniture. Mary sat in the small kitchen, a knife in her hand and a pile of potatoes on the table ahead of her.

The door was open but there wasn't a window to pull out the stove's heat. The room was stifling, gloomy.

"Well?" Mrs. Moon said. Mary got up and walked to the stove. She fussed with the soup, her back turned to us.

"I didn't find him. I waited but he didn't come."

Mary turned to her mother. They exchanged a glance that I couldn't interpret. A shoulder slightly lifted, a tilt of the head—gestures that a lifetime together had built into a language.

"I'm going tomorrow with Kropp," I said.

Mary turned back to the stove. Mrs. Moon stood silently, looking at me but seeing all the weak-willed men who had never given her what she wanted.

"You might as well stay here for supper," Mrs. Moon said finally, bringing me back into focus. "There's no sense me running back to the rectory later."

I'd rather have starved than eat there. The kitchen was like a boiler room, purgatorial. Mrs. Moon did not seem to perspire; instead, her cheeks turned scarlet and her nose went to purple, the tiny veins throbbing close to the surface. Her rage had turned inward, simmering in a way that only she fully understood. In comparison Mary seemed reduced, empty. Mary's hair was pinned roughly to the top of her head and her neck was glazed with sweat. She wore a shabby dress with splitting seams.

"I could cut something up for you," I offered, pulling out a chair.

"Probably just yourself," Mrs. Moon snapped. "Find the boys and bring them in. That ought to be enough for you."

In the backyard a garden was started, the frail tomatoes and peas and potatoes struggling to stand erect. Lettuce and spinach already grew thick. A calico cat prowled through a low wall of rhubarb that thrived beside a chicken coop.

As I watched a knife flew over the cat's head, slashing through a rhubarb leaf. The cat shot into a clump of lilacs.

I found Mary's boys behind the coop.

"What are you doing?"

"Nothing."

"Nothing," Mike said, surly, as though blaming me for something he did not quite comprehend. "There ain't nothing to do here."

"Nothing?"

"Why?"

"What about the cat?"

He ignored me. Gabe went to retrieve the knife.

"What about Pentz?" Mike said, angry. "What did he say when you found him?" He dared me to lie, his eyes burning in a face raw with acne.

"It's time for supper."

"What did he say?"

"It's time for us to eat."

"That's not what he said."

I took them by the shoulders and steered them toward the house. They both twisted loose and hurried ahead. When I entered the room they were already at the table.

We sat together in the kitchen, each of us staring into our bowl of soup. I led a prayer, something about hope and sustenance and the grace of God. Spoons clattered against the bowls. The fire died in the stove, the embers crackling.

"You didn't see anything of him," Mary asked me.

"I went through . . ."

Mrs. Moon interrupted. "Let it be."

"Let him tell," Gabe said, looking at his mother. Her eyes dropped back to her soup.

"Quiet, I said," Mrs. Moon hissed. She glared at Gabe.

"I'll kill him," he said to himself. Mrs. Moon looked at him appraisingly, her lips pursed.

The rest of the meal passed in near silence. Pass the butter. More soup? I'll get you coffee. Delicious. All of it. Empty words. When I stood out on the grass again I felt like a criminal finally set free.

I'LL TELL YOU ABOUT THE DREAM I HAD THAT NIGHT, AND then not another word on the subject. I talk about my dreams and I get confused. I end up wondering what really happened and what I dreamed. I don't need that trouble on top of everything else. I can live in the past, I can even see the advantage of it. But I won't live in a dream world, not yet. My life is devalued when I get mixed up.

I dreamed I walked up the street toward the church. A pair of pigeons dove from the steeple. The bell rang faintly. Two heads craned out of the slats in the steeple window. Mary's boys.

I opened the church door and slipped inside, creeping up the choir loft stairs, hoping to trap them. I squeezed the knob of the door leading to the attic and turned it slowly. I heard nothing but my breath and the sigh of the wooden floor.

In the attic a pigeon flapped, stirring the gray dust. I started up the ladder to the steeple. The trapdoor at the ladder's last rung was skewed. A wedge of sunlight fell down the steeple shaft.

As I reached the top I heard a scream. The ladder shook. I fell against it, clutching the raw wood. A vague shape streaked out the steeple door.

I ran down the ladder and dashed into the attic again. Nothing.

Behind me the door slammed. Feet smacked against the stairs. I twisted at the doorknob but it spun uselessly. I was trapped.

The floorboards trembled beneath my feet. The sound I heard vibrated at the threshold of hearing, vast and empty and hollow, the sound of everything that does not exist.

I rattled the knob desperately, my chest tightening with the pressure of the sound, every breath seemingly the last I could manage. Suddenly the shaft caught against the latch. As I stumbled down the stairs the sound ebbed and died.

The choir loft was abandoned. A lamp lit the organ keys. A black pebble was set on the lowest note and the bellows flapped loosely. I thought I heard more footsteps against the stairs, but they were faint, indefinite. I was alone.

SUNDAY

LET ME STOP HERE, BARELY A MILE FROM OLD ST. JUDE, AND describe for you the lay of the land. The road is a two-lane blacktop with steep shoulders and treacherous curves. The sun, still rising, is at our backs. On the right the lake, royal blue, glitters with the early sun. The trees are oak, elm, ash, and Russian olive. Sumac is clustered on the north side of the hills. There, to the left, is a pasture populated by cows that loll on the eastern slopes. Beyond the pasture is a field of corn, the first tassels waving in the breeze, and further still, enclosed by a windbreak of tall pine, a farmstead. And clouds, cumulus clouds that rise like mountains, white and purple and gray. The whole of it etched on the tired cells of my brain, the memory slumbering beside what I see, this day and a thousand others tangled together like young lovers.

Schneider drives us past the first sign of my town. "St. Jude," he reads aloud. "Building Permits Required."

"Looks friendly," Schneider says. I ignore him. Sad to say, he enjoys the luxury of believing me too deaf to hear.

"Pull over," I tell him. He makes a great show of consulting his watch.

"Thirteen minutes to get to church," Schneider says, poking at the buttons that bristle from his wrist. We veer toward the ditch. "Whoops," he says, laughing as he cranks the wheel. My head snaps from side to side.

114

Won't that be the day, when the skin hangs on Schneider's bones, when every step is agony? Of course he can't imagine it. He'll be young forever, that's what he thinks, even though a powerful argument to the contrary, yours truly, is hunched over beside him. My spine is like a noodle these days. With each mile I sink further in my seat, held in place finally by the shoulder harness that cuts across my throat.

If, after all, the Hindus are right, then I pray I come back as the nurse who connects the doddering Schneider's catheter. Or even as the aide who empties his colostomy bag. Anything just to watch as Schneider's eyes are opened.

"Right here," I tell him. "Pull over."

"Here? Now?"

"So we miss an epistle. I'll recite thirty for you on the way home." If I'm damned for missing a part of one mass there's less justice than I think. I don't rule out the possibility.

We bounce over the gravel and pull up under an elm near the ballroom. The lake shimmers, scored by the light wind. St. Jude's churches poke through the trees on the far shore.

"This is the ballroom?" Schneider asks. "Where what's-her-name got married? It looks like a machine shed."

I'm pained to admit he's right. Naturally I resent him for it. My usual habitat—have I already said this?—is the warm water of memory, where things are what they were as much as what they have become. Unless provoked I don't see what Schneider sees. I remember the moon, I feel the breeze off the lake. The ballroom walls are built from rounded logs and the light is a golden glow. But in fact the log building burned fifteen years ago, about the same time the polka crowd got too old to dance. "Suspicious," the investigators said, but in the end they paid up. The owners built a metal barn for rock 'n' roll and pocketed the difference.

Schneider stabs his watch again. "We'll get to church," I tell him. He looks dubious.

"It's a mortal sin," he says.

" 'The Sabbath was made for man, not man for the Sabbath.' Mark, if you want to look it up."

"But . . ."

"I'll hear your confession on the way home."

In his anxiety and boredom Schneider fidgets with the dashboard buttons. The emergency lights flash. A stream of cleaner shoots against the windshield. Poor Schneider. He needs more stimulation than I can provide.

What do I expect? The papers fill him to overflowing with news of washing machine murders and sex torture with heated knifes. I'm out of my league. A modest romance nipped in the bud. A jilted lover who disappears. An angry son. Big deal. Have you heard about the porn ring in the next town over? Children—I'm not making this up—were debauched by their own parents. Mommy and daddy held the shaking cameras. That's what I'm up against.

I want to shout into Schneider's ear that life wasn't always as it is. My little town couldn't ignore even its smallest wounds. It bled, it picked at the scabs. Now the world is spinning crooked. On the worse days I believe that if forced to live solely in the present I'd die before the sun set.

"Let me finish," I tell Schneider.

He slips down in his seat, defeated.

MRS. MOON TRAPPED ME IN THE HALLWAY THAT MORNING as I lurched from my bed to the bathroom. She must have been waiting.

"So now that we're alone tell me," she said. "What you saw."

"I thought you weren't interested."

"I tell you I want to know."

"There isn't anything to tell. Alois wasn't there."

"No sign at all?"

"That's what I said. He wasn't there."

She stopped to think. "Good," she said.

"Good?"

"If I never see him again I'll be happy."

My intestines rumbled. The smell of something burning drifted from the kitchen. It was heavy and cloying, sickening to my empty stomach.

"Is there something you need to check?" I asked, nodding toward the kitchen. I wanted to get away from her.

"I don't need you telling me how to cook," she replied, glaring.

"This isn't the end of the world."

"What do you know? You been here a week." The hard edge of her expression collapsed. She covered her face and hurried into the kitchen. I waited a moment before following her.

The kitchen was her creation; a disorderly world filled with dirty dishes and dusted with flour. She stood at the window fingering her rosary beads, more Muslim than Christian in this. I put a hand on her shoulder and she flinched.

"What are you praying for?"

"I don't want to know what happened," she said. "It ain't going to help. I don't want to know the worst. I don't want it to eat at me night after night."

"You don't usually need to pray for ignorance."

"It wasn't him alone. She let him, just like the priest. And now she lies about it. I know. I can see it on her. This time I'm not making excuses. I'm not telling anybody anything. I'm not letting her get at me this way. I won't let her do it again."

"What about Mary?"

"Let it sit in her stomach. She can take care of herself this time." The beads clattered in her hands.

"Maybe she already told you the truth," I said.

"God have mercy on you."

She laughed, joyless. The birds outside the window sang. Someone shouted my name.

Mrs. Moon marched to the door and flung it open. Lieber stood there, sweating, anxious.

"What's the matter with you?" Mrs. Moon demanded.

"The baptism," Lieber croaked, breathless. "We wait now for the priest."

MARTHA, LIEBER'S WIFE, HELD THE BABY, A GIRL WITH A lock of blond hair that curled across her forehead. Her eyes were the color of robin eggs. I saw so little of Lieber in her that I wondered whether Mrs. Moon was right. Could he be the father?

"She's perfect," I said.

"Dolores Elaine the name is," Lieber whispered, smoothing the long, white baptism dress. "The godfather you already know, Mayor Krank. Someday, God forbid she should be so desperate, her husband gets a city job."

"And here," Lieber said, "the godmother." He gestured toward a woman with bulging, ruddy cheeks. St. Jude was a fat-cheeked town. She smiled and her eyes disappeared. "My wife's sister, Ruth."

I led the family to the baptismal font that stood beside the confessional. The font was cut of marble, cool on the hottest days. Lieber stuck his little finger into the cruet that held the holy water. "Wait," he said, "it's too cold."

"It's no different than it ever is," Krank argued.

"For a minute in the sun we warm it."

"It's better cold," said Krank, baiting Lieber as instinctively as he breathed. "They hear the baby cry in heaven."

The grocer pointed at Krank, exasperated. "A frozen brain for the baby this godfather wants."

"Honey, please," his wife said. "Not today." Lieber settled back on his heels.

I motioned the mother closer to the font and pushed the blanket away from her baby's head. The others crowded around us. Do you renounce Satan and all his works, I asked.

The baby's gown shone in the shadows. We could have been Adam's family, gathered around the only fire on earth.

"Yes," they said, "we do renounce him." The baby gurgled and closed its eyes.

Do you renounce the vanities of the world, the false treasure of riches and pleasure, the corrupt teachings and the sin?

Yes, said Krank and Ruth. I do. I do. Despite the chill, the baby fell asleep.

Her head was impossibly soft to the touch. "I baptize you in the name of the Father, and of the Son, and of the Holy Ghost," I said, trickling water from the cruet onto her head.

Her skull pulsed with the flow of blood. The water ran over the unjoined bones and the fine hair and splashed against the cold stone. The baby howled, her pink fists pounding at the air.

"I told you," Lieber whispered angrily.

Krank laughed. The mother ignored them both. She looked down at her child, rocking it back and forth, repeating its name as gently as a prayer. One of her tears splashed on the baby's face as she dabbed at its eyes. She dried her own face with the baby's blanket and walked away, her sister at her side. Krank and Lieber's perpetual argument raged over the baptismal font.

The oldest and sickliest of my parishioners already huddled in their pews, daydreaming as they pretended to pray. I hurried to the sacristy to prepare for mass.

Krank called after me. "What do you hear about Alois?"

I kept walking.

YESTERDAY, THE DAY BEFORE. MY BRAIN ACHES WHEN I TRY to remember. The nurse wakes me and I eat a meal cooked from—what?—cardboard? I struggle to walk, as though I were a baby again. Then I watch my brothers in faith drool and burble as we sit together in front of our television. One of them, a Father McDeavitt, by all accounts a pious man, spends his days screaming obscenities. Father Marshall, not a day over seventy, pounds his coffee cup endlessly against the chair to which he's tied. Then there's Jacobsen, always lacking something. "Get me my slippers," he says. "Turn up the heat. Get me a deck of cards." The nurses roll their eyes and do his bidding, killing him with kindness. He's itching for an argument, and they won't give him the pleasure. Nuts, I thought at first, all of them absolutely insane. Now I wonder. Are their memories as vivid as mine? Do they look at me, sullen, aloof, and judge me every bit as crazy?

The past is an altogether more agreeable place for those of

us still able to imagine it. Am I repeating myself? So what? I
regard senility as a matter of choice and repetition as one of
its prerogatives.

THE EXACT MOMENT MY SERMON BEGAN THAT SUNDAY, NOW
there's a barnacle fixed deep in my brain. The oak pulpit, the
deep wood grain oiled by decades of nervous hands; the page
of handwritten notes, soggy with sweat. I remember even
though I'd rather forget.

Oh, I had plans. A simple sermon, a familiar point. John
8:7, brothers and sisters in Christ. The scribes and Pharisees
brought to Him the adultress taken in the very act. Such
should be stoned, they said, rocks in hand. Full of piety,
panting for blood. And what did Christ do? Run to get
Himself a sharp stone? Who remembers what He said?

Silence of course, guilty, simpering silence.

Christ told the hypocrites, Let he who is without sin cast
the first stone! Yes, yes! Does this strike close to home,
brothers and sisters? Can you help but squirm with recognition?

What choice do you have but to shut your slandering
mouths? What choice but to live your miserable lives and to
let Alois and Mary live theirs?

If only the scribes and Pharisees had filled my church. I
was confronted by a parish thick-skinned and rock-brained.
"They brought to Him the adultress," I said, then watched
as Smit the undertaker touched a finger to his tongue, polish-
ing each of his black buttons with a drop of spittle. Kropp
cleaned his nails with a pocket knife. Heads lolled and babies
wailed.

Even as I made my arguments I could hear them refuted.
What if the town didn't rise up to defend itself, to attack the
lazy and morally lax? What if every field were left to weeds
and every barn came tumbling down? What if passion consis-
tently outweighed common sense in St. Jude? I'd be eating
bark with the rest of them while the church roof fell.

I mumbled, I sweated, I lost my place. My sphincter,
mischievous, loosened itself. I watched fifty heads track the

flight of a bird trapped in the church while fifty more rested against the cool plaster wall.

"Let he who is without sin cast the first stone," I said. A hundred mouths yawned in reply.

When at last the mass was ended my herd staggered to its feet. "*Credo in unum Deum*," I said, "*Patrem omnipotentem, factorem caeli et terrae.*" Latin, English, it made no difference: the same dull glaze covered their features. When the final organ note died they stampeded for the doors.

As I watched them flee something Mrs. Moon said came back to me. Mary and the priest. So finally she admitted it.

KROPP PERCHED ON THE FENDER OF HIS PATROL CAR, A failing patriarch. His nostrils flared. His good ear tilted toward the sky. He shaded his fogged eyes against the light and craned his head. All that he sought seemed just beyond his ability to see and hear and smell.

"Got any leads," I called to him.

Kropp studied me quizzically. "Oh, ja," he said. There was no chance he had heard. "We'll be back long before then."

He stretched out the kinks in his back and limped toward the door. "We go," he said. I climbed in beside him.

Kropp drove more from memory than recognition. He leaned toward the windshield, squinting to make out shapes on the road.

"What if we don't find him today," I shouted.

"Where else could he be?" We sped through a stop sign.

"Just suppose."

"He got animals. He can't leave them."

As our speed increased the distance between Kropp's nose and the windshield narrowed. Gravel shot off the car's underside.

"What if we find him?" I asked. Kropp turned to me, ignoring the road.

"What?"

"If we find him."

"We get to the bottom. We find out what happened." He

glanced at the road to pull the car around a curve, then turned back to me. "Last night at the ball game," he shouted. "Boy from Jordan slid into home. Dust everywhere. Couldn't see. What do I do? Scratch my head and wonder what happened? Say we're better off if we don't know? Called him out. Just like they call our boys out when we play there. Didn't have to think about it. It was decided. People want things settled. So they know what to think."

We shot past the depot. The same train that brought me the week before had just arrived, an hour and a half late. "You see the conductor?" Kropp asked. He stood on the platform, combing through his mustache with his fingers. Beside the train he seemed insignificant.

"Sure I see him."

"The old liar with the mustache, that one?" Kropp asked.

"That's him."

Kropp waved. "My brother," he said. He swung the car onto the gravel road that led out of town.

The car filled with dust. Everything around us was lush and green and still we choked. Kropp's nose and eyes ran, dripping on his shirt. "The dust," he said, waving his hand at the cloud in front of his face. "These dirt roads. They're killing me."

He charged over the hill that hid Alois's farm and down into the shallow valley, past the drive. "It's right around here," Kropp said, grinding his eyes with the back of his hand.

"I think . . ." I said.

"Ach," he declared. "Why don't you tell me?" He slammed down the brakes and threw the car into reverse.

We bumped over the path, the donkey's howl drowned by the noise of Kropp's car. He pulled into the farmyard and cut the engine. Animals screamed at us from every direction.

"Don't sound like he's been here," Kropp said.

Kropp tipped his head back and cupped his hands around his mouth. "Alois!" he shouted. "Alois Pentz!"

Silence.

He turned to me. "Checked the barn?"

I shook my head.

"Found Fedner in his barn. Two years ago. Bad year for corn. The fungus. Wife thought he disappeared."

"He was hiding there?"

Kropp stopped and stared at me. "Well, I suppose nobody told you yet," he said finally. "Hung himself. And the next year was beautiful for corn. Too bad he didn't wait."

"Didn't know how to rest. Didn't have any idea. Always in a hurry. As a boy even. Skipped seventh grade and went right on to eighth. I went to school with him you know," he said, introducing an astonishing thought: Kropp as a child.

He marched up the dirt ramp to the barn's big sliding doors. I watched, rooted to the spot, looking over the sweep of land. Wasn't it too beautiful for such misery? The great fields of corn, the impenetrable swamps, the woods and smooth pastures—how could happiness be subverted here?

Kropp leaned against the barn door. It didn't budge. He motioned to me. We pushed together. The door shivered, then broke loose of the rust that held it in place.

Light from a window set high on the wall fell over a mountain of alfalfa, still green and fragrant. A rope dangled from the ceiling. I prayed, more for myself than for Alois.

"Nothing here," Kropp said. He opened a trapdoor and lowered himself through the floor.

The smell of manure and ammonia rose around me as I followed, stepping off the ladder into a bed of oozing straw. In the dim light liquid eyes shone. Alois's herd lumbered toward me. They appeared neither desperate nor angry, just dumbly persistent, as though a thought that had taken days to form would now take months to dissipate. I scrambled over the low wood wall that enclosed them.

"Hungry," Kropp said, throwing a bale of alfalfa to the cows. They circled and tore at it with their dull teeth. Milk dripped from their teats. Kropp headed toward Alois's lake.

The water reflected the trees, the clouds, the sky. The red boat drifted on the water as it had the day before. But now a naked boy stood on either end. They dove when they saw us. I don't know how Kropp saw them.

"Bring the boat here," he shouted, striving to make up for his dim senses with his power of speech. The words rang on the opposite bank, raising a flock of sparrows from the trees. The boys pulled themselves back into the boat and rowed lazily toward shore. As they came closer I recognized them as Mary's boys.

Of course. Omnipresent, omniscient, inheritors of all Mrs. Moon's worst traits. I thought of them as demons, not children. They rowed toward us with no sense of surprise or hurry, as though they had expected us and wondered why we had kept them waiting.

Kropp charged down the slope toward them, kicking aside the alfalfa. Just as suddenly he stopped. Teeth shone from the shadow beneath the willow. Alois's dog still waited. Kropp eased toward the shore. The dog disappeared further beneath the tree. We watched silently as the boys approached.

The boat's hull scraped against the muck. The boys jumped onto the grass. Water dripped from their naked limbs. Their hair was plastered against their heads.

"What do you want?" Gabe said. His tone suggested that Kropp better have a good answer.

"This is your boat?" Kropp said.

"It ain't," Gabe said.

"Then you stole it?"

"We rescued it. It was floating loose and we brought it back."

Kropp peered inside the boat. "And you lost the anchor while you were at it."

"It didn't have none when we found it," Gabe replied, examining the boat himself. "I didn't think nothing of it."

I remembered watching Alois's homemade anchor disappear in the black water, the rope trailing along behind it. "He had one," I said. "I think he had one."

Kropp turned to me. "You been in his boat?"

"We went swimming."

He looked blank.

"Swimming," I shouted.

He nodded. "Show me where."

I remember the groan of the oars above all else. Anything might bring it back—an unoiled door hinge, a rusted nail pulled from hard wood. This is the shorthand by which my memory works. I hear the sound and I feel uncertain, remorseful, afraid. Kropp pulled at the splintered handles, and the rusty oarlocks whimpered. The noise resonated inside the boat's wooden hull, primitive instrument, then echoed again from the lake's surface. The awful music quieted us all. From the bow I watched Kropp, his feet splayed before him, his crooked back lunging forward with each pull. The boys shivered beside each other in the stern, still naked, their hands clasped between their thighs.

"Over there," I told Kropp, gesturing vaguely. He grunted and the oars wailed again in their locks.

"Start looking," Kropp commanded.

"For what?" I asked, willfully confused.

He held the oars above the water. They dripped, the water rippling the surface. Kropp turned toward me, one dull eye taking my measure. "For the body," he said.

I crouched in the bow, looking into the lake. I saw the reflection of my own face distorted by the curl of water pushed before the hull. The water was black, the lake's bottom so distant it seemed not to exist.

"This far?" Kropp said.

There was no way to tell. "I don't think so. I don't know."

With a pair of quick strokes Kropp turned the boat around. He was like a farmer tilling the open prairie, cutting back and forth in parallel rows, imposing order where none had existed. I strained to see beyond my own face and the sun's glare into the blackness. When still I saw nothing I struggled to imagine all that might exist beneath us. Sunfish slipping among the weeds, snails crawling in the soft, black silt. An anchor, a rope, a body. It couldn't be.

Kropp plowed his furrow and turned again. "Could be in one of those trees," he said. "Laughing at us. Could be twenty miles from here."

The slow creak of the oars tied a knot deep in my head.

Each stroke pulled it tighter, left me more eager to trade Alois's corpse for an end to the search.

He's not in the lake, I told myself. There isn't any reason. Nothing happened, not really. Mary said so. Let her mother think whatever she wished. Nothing happened between Mary and Alois. Nothing happened between Mary and Unger. Life can go on the way it always has.

And even if Kropp were right, we would never find Alois. Not by peering over the gunwale of Alois's boat and staring into nothingness.

I SAY THE WATER WAS BLACK, BUT THAT ISN'T PRECISELY true. Below the reflective surface, specks of algae—thousands of them, millions—were swept along by subtle currents, tinting the lake with the color of life. Deeper still, where light could no longer penetrate, there the water was black. Blacker even than my cassock, which is so often covered now with crumbs and lint.

Blacker than death? We'll all find out soon enough, won't we? I've read newspaper stories about people who die and live to tell about it, people resuscitated after a heart attack, that sort of thing. The near-dead say they see lights glowing at the end of a tunnel, lights that pull their souls away from their faltering carcasses. I repeat that the lake, ultimately, was black. If the water was blacker than death, then so be it.

"WHAT'S THAT?"

Gabe's voice was flat, matter of fact. He poked a finger down through the lake's surface, pointing. Kropp dug the oars in, struggling to stop the boat.

"I don't see nothing," Mike claimed. He leaned over Gabe's shoulder. Their naked bodies were tense, motionless. "You're lying," he said.

"Way down. It's white. Way down there."

"Throw the anchor," Kropp ordered.

"There isn't any," I reminded him.

"Christ," Kropp moaned. The oars floated loose, chirping in the locks. He was on his feet, looking down into the water beside the boys. I got up to join them and the boat lurched.

"Sit down," Kropp said. His scalp twitched as he tried to make out the shape in the water.

"I can dive down there," Gabe volunteered.

"What if it's dead?" Mike said.

"So?"

"You all sit down," Kropp shouted.

They settled reluctantly on the wood plank. "I still say you didn't see nothing," Mike sneered.

"Quiet!" Kropp thundered.

He kicked off his shoes, peeled off his clothes. Kropp's buttocks sagged and his belly bulged. His skin was hairless. Balanced on his spindly white legs Kropp looked like a massive heron. He made a sign of the cross and jumped, vanishing beneath the roiled surface.

As it calmed we saw his misshapen image, his arms and legs flailing at the water. The air he expelled rose in bubbles and the bubbles burst back into the fresh air. I stood behind the boys, braced against the muscles that trembled under their clammy skin.

"He looks like a big carp down there," Gabe said.

Mike laughed. "Yeah. But he ain't gonna find nothing."

"You can see it plain," Gabe argued.

If you looked long enough into the dark water anything became visible. Wasn't that it, there: a pale shape, tethered, floating halfway between the surface and the bottom? Then the water bent the light again and it vanished, a ghost.

Kropp was gone. Bubbles, fewer and fewer, boiled up into the air. We looked down into the darkness where imagination is all that remains.

Without warning Kropp burst to the surface behind us, wheezing as he filled his lungs with air. His face was the color of a thing that has never seen the sun. He clutched the side of the boat and gasped, "In my pocket. A knife."

Gabe rummaged through Kropp's pants. "What's down there?" he asked.

Kropp grabbed the knife from his hand and gulped at the air again. His chest swelled, his cheeks bulged. He sank into the water.

Far up above us a hawk circled on a current of air. It climbed in a lazy orbit, disappearing in the sky. Water spiders walked across the lake's surface. In the shallows a fish jumped.

"Look," Gabe said.

Kropp ascended.

He broke the surface, treading water with his right hand. The fringe of hair was slicked against his skull. He threw the knife into the boat and grabbed the gunwale. Kropp's left arm was wrapped around Alois's naked corpse.

The body was inflated with gases. Alois was smooth and plump, like a newborn. The anchor rope Kropp cut was still tied around his neck. I couldn't see his face.

"He's so cold," Kropp said, expressionless. He pulled himself out of the water, hooking a toe on the side and flopping into the boat. Water pooled at his feet.

"Like a balloon," Kropp said. The body floated beside the boat face down. "Grab him under the arm. We'll pull him in."

The boys didn't move. "Can't we tow him?" I said. I hadn't seen a body before that wasn't in a casket.

"Under the arm," Kropp said, as if he hadn't heard.

We knelt in the stern and pulled Alois's torso out of the water. His head fell face down to the boat's bottom. His legs still trailed in the water.

"That's good enough," Kropp said. Naked, he settled back to the oars. The boys cowered in the bow.

Alois's feet jittered in the water as Kropp rowed. A pair of dragonflies settled on his back.

When the boat touched the weeds the boys bolted, grabbing their clothes and vanishing over the rise. Alois's dog waded in the water, poking at the still foot with his snout, his nose twitching. The animal sighed and returned to the shadows under the willow.

Kropp and I picked up the body, sinking deep into the muck under its weight. We set him on the grass, the swollen limbs akimbo. Grit from the boat's bottom was pushed into his face.

I tried to straighten his arms and legs. "I'll get the car," Kropp said. He pulled on his clothes and lumbered up the hill, leaving me alone with the body. I brushed the dirt from Alois's brow and smoothed his hair. His eyes were still open, staring dully into the sky. I moved up the rise to wait.

Kropp's car rattled over the hill. He drove past me down to the lake. When he killed the engine the silence was overwhelming.

Kropp leaned on the open door, looking over the lake. I walked down the slope. We stood together without speaking.

Kropp coughed and slammed the door. "You want to give him the last prayers?" he said.

I hadn't thought of it. If I couldn't help the living, then what could I do for the dead? I wished I had never left the city.

"Suicide," I said finally. "I don't know."

Kropp looked at me, straining to see. He turned and walked toward Alois. "Then help me load him up," he said.

We wrapped the body in a bright red blanket Kropp pulled from the trunk. The blanket was too short to cover the bloated feet. "That's good enough," Kropp said impatiently. As we slid Alois across the back seat he seemed to groan.

"The gases," Kropp said, slamming the door. The car bounced over the field, past the farmhouse. Kropp leaned over the wheel.

We sped past the fields and pastures and the few houses set back in the hills. Dust filled the car again.

"Why did he do it?" I asked Kropp.

"Wide? What?" he said, grimacing as he tried to understand.

"Drown himself," I shouted. "Why?"

"How could he live here? After what he done."

"What do we know for sure? What if he was murdered?"

Kropp shrugged. "You want it both ways."

Everything we passed was ripe, green, blooming. The birds that watched from the wires sang and the back seat springs squeaked at every dip in the road. Neither Kropp nor I said another word until we stopped behind Smit's shop and asked to see the undertaker.

THE BURIAL

"THAT'S IT?" SAYS SCHNEIDER, HOPEFUL. BEFORE I CAN answer he starts the car. With a modest screech of tires— nothing excessive, not for thin-blooded Schneider—we're off. We skim along the lake's edge, climbing the big hill.

"Turn here," I tell Schneider.

"Here?"

"A shortcut." A lie, but a small one.

"You're sure?"

"Take it."

The gravel road swings wide of the town, carrying us out into the country. Schneider drums on the steering wheel, realizing he's been had.

Corn covers the hillsides, an army in close ranks. "Beautiful," I say.

Schneider stews.

"Look over there," I tell him.

"What?"

"There."

"That apartment?"

OAKRIDGE, the sign says. ELEGANT COUNTRY LIVING. The house and barn and broken-down implements are gone. The management, I'm told, hauled in sand to make a beach. I'm not arguing against progress. I'm not saying Alois deserved

a museum. But this place defiles the past. The brochure hints
at a ghost in the lake.

"What about it?" Schneider says.

"Nothing," I say. I give up, at least for now. I can't do all
his thinking for him.

We head toward town through the subdivision that has
spread onto the far side of the highway. For decades nothing
but the feed mill occupied this strip. Now the mill is abandoned. A circuit-board factory thrives. A motel just opened,
and a new chain-operated hamburger stand seems to sprout
up every week. My town is finally inseparable from all the
others. Even the Lutheran church is gone. The Lutherans
erected a pile of bricks on a hill overlooking the highway,
then rented the old church to a series of cults and funda-
mentalists. When the postal service made them an offer they
jumped at the chance to tear the place down.

Schneider loads me into my wheelchair and pushes me into
the churchyard. I can describe every groove in the stone steps,
every dip worn by a thousand feet over a hundred years. And
what difference does it make? I can't climb them now anyway.
Blinding pain shoots through my hip whenever I left my leg.

Schneider rolls me up the handicapped ramp. What I save
in pain I pay for with pride. Heads turn. I hear my name
whispered. The church is full; the mass has long since begun.
An usher—he seems inflated, like one of Lieber's boys—shakes
my hand. "Never looked better," he claims. I call him a liar
and he laughs. The new priest, a child named Kinter, starts
his sermon.

He seems to be speaking about grace though it's hard to
say for sure. His voice is as lulling as a breeze.

It makes no earthly difference what he says. God still
exists and the living can't know Him and the dead remain
dead. Kinter's voice is a pleasant drone. In the back of my
head I hear dirt grate against a shovel.

WITHOUT ALOIS, SMIT WAS LEFT ALONE TO FILL THE GRAVE.
I offered to help.

"That was a real decent funeral," Smit said. He leaned against his shovel and lit a cigarette. I nodded and threw a load of black dirt into the hole, listening to it rap against the plain wood coffin.

Lieber had rounded up the six pallbearers who carried Alois's body. They wound through the orchard to the cemetery, ducking beneath the low branches. I led the procession, swinging a censer filled with smouldering incense. "May the angels lead thee into paradise," I sang. "May the martyrs receive thee at thy coming." The smoke curled up into the leaves and was gone.

Alois never had more friends than he did that day. Half the parish showed up, just as Kropp predicted.

He appeared at my window late Sunday night, tapping on the screen. "Hey," he whispered. I was already asleep. "Hey," he said, louder.

I shot upright, pulling the sheet around me. "What is it?" I said. "Who's there?" Kropp pushed his face against the screen.

"We should decide," he said.

"What?"

"What killed Alois."

I got out of bed and crouched next to the window. Kropp stood less than a foot from me. He cupped his hands over his eyes and pressed close to the screen.

"What killed Alois."

"We don't know?" I said. "You found him. You cut the rope."

"The rope, ja," Kropp said. "But you can't say for sure."

"Can't say what for sure? He tied the rope around his neck and jumped in the lake and we found him. What can't we say for sure?"

"Speak up," Kropp insisted. He pressed his ear against the screen.

"We know what happened!"

"So you won't bury him," Kropp said. "A suicide." Then I understood.

I'd sat for hours, watching the gnats that circled the desk

light. How could he be dead? I still saw his face, full of the setting sun. I hadn't considered his burial.

"There are laws," I said.

"What does that mean?"

"Church laws. About who I can bury."

Kropp stepped back from the window and let his arms sweep over his head, drawing in the entire town. "Here! Alone! All of us together! Alone. Alone! Before anything else we got to watch out for each other." He banged against the window frame with his fist.

"Quiet," I whispered. "Please."

"What's your answer?" His few strands of hair stood on end.

"I'll . . . I don't know. Well," I said.

"Ja?"

"I'll pray on it."

"Ahh," he said, disgusted. "We make out the death certificate tomorrow," he said. "Suicide. Sounds like what happens in the city. Like we don't take care of our own. Who knows but God? That it wasn't an accident?" He turned and vanished in the darkness.

I prayed for an answer but the heavens didn't part. I lay wide-eyed in my bed, arguing with myself.

WHO'S TO SAY HE WAS WRONG TO KILL HIMSELF? HOW CAN WE judge?

Life isn't a gift we can return. We have an obligation to use it as well as we're able.

Some gift! What kind of bully gives you a present you're forced to use? Who calls that a gift?

We're obliged to give thanks for this magnificent gift. This magnificent gift of life. Alois had no right to refuse. What he did is no different than murder.

Magnificent gift? Is this a joke? What kind of bonehead am I arguing with? Since when is it magnificent to be stupid and alone and living in squalor? What did he have to be thankful

*for? He was an exile. He cried out alone and no one com-
forted him.*

*Listen, we have the body and the rope. The facts speak
for themselves.*

*So what, that's what I'm saying. So what? Is it less sinful
to withhold love from those who most need it? Who in this
town is innocent?*

*Can we will ourselves to love? Can we control the beating
of our hearts?*

I woke up tangled in my sheets, the sun already risen. I
threw on my clothes and went to Kropp's office.

"We'll put him in the church cemetery and let God decide," I said.

"We put down 'accidental drowning' then." Kropp pumped
my hand, welcoming me to his tribe.

"MAY HIS SOUL AND THE SOULS OF ALL THE FAITHFUL DE-
parted, through the mercy of God, rest in peace," I said. His
neighbors murmured amen and went back to their shops and
farms.

Lieber passed me on his way out of the cemetery. "We
thank you, Father," he said, avoiding my eyes.

Mary Moon touched my elbow. She spoke so softly I had
to bow my head to understand. "I told the truth about what
happened," she said. "There ain't nothing more to it than
that."

"Nobody blames you."

"You don't know," she said, and hurried away.

Mrs. Moon stood on the kitchen steps, watching. When
the body was lowered she spit in the grass and let the door
slam.

LATE THAT SUMMER MARY SEEMED SWOLLEN, HAGGARD. SHE
wore loose clothes and moved slowly. Then, in the space of
a few days, she returned to normal. Miscarriage, the parish
busybodies confided to me in a hush. They pleaded with me

to set her straight. "Her morals," they said. "We can't even say for sure whose baby it is."

"First remove the mote from your own eye," I responded, wishing I could turn them into pillars of salt. I had no idea of what I might say to Mary. I didn't ask what happened and she didn't tell me. I guessed that the child was Unger's.

Her boys spread the story that Alois killed himself. His lake became a haunted site, a spot where all their anxiety was focused. The town's children went there on warm summer nights, stripped off their clothes, stepped through the ooze, and dove into the dark water. When they heard a fish jump from the water in the night, they panicked. The down rose on their bare backs and they rushed for shore, grabbing their clothes, running naked through the fields, thankful for their fear.

YOUNG KINTER'S VOICE IS BEAUTIFUL. IT MAKES NO DIFFER-ence what he says. I dream and dream and dream.

"The mass is ended," he says, "go in peace." Schneider nudges me and rolls the wheelchair toward the door.

"I agree with what he said in his homily, basically," Schneider says. I start looking for a face I recognize.

We'll stay to visit the young fool who now occupies my office, and he and Schneider can go talk about all the things that don't matter. With any luck Mary Moon will invite us to stay at the rectory for lunch. She is, after all, her mother's child. She'll cook as though I were Christ resurrected. Ham, certainly, and maybe a chicken, mashed potatoes and rivers of gravy, steaming bread and raspberry jam. I haven't been so hungry in years.

She is thicker now, and the luster is gone from her hair. The stories about her stopped years ago. Only a few old-timers remember them, and no one believes what they say. They're too old to be trusted.

We'll eat and talk until the sun hangs on the horizon and the fields are lit by the hand of God. Then, when I can no longer offer another reason for delay, Schneider will haul me back to my prison again. During the drive I plan to bend his ear. There's more than one story on my mind.

I swear to you, there are moments when I remember everything. The creak of my shoe as I left Mrs. Moon's deathbed; the inexpressible pain in Lieber's eyes the day his child died; Unger's fervent reply when I asked him. "Was the sin worth the pleasure?"

"Yes," he croaked from his nursing home bed. "Oh, yes. Oh, yes."

Despite all I remember still I know nothing at all. To imagine the longings of a thousand souls is more than one life's work. It's an infinite job.

I could live here forever.